As they drew up behind the limo at the exit booth, their driver glanced back over his shoulder. "Successful evening, ladies?"

Before either could answer, he gave a grunt and slumped against the Huntling Security guard. Carol didn't need to hear the flat crack, see the spray of blood or the hole in the windscreen. "Get down!"

"Jesus!" said the guard beside the driver. "Oh, Jesus!" Another crack split the air, and he was silent.

Carol had shoved Marla onto the floor and lay over her. A handgun was useless in this situation, but the cold weight of it in her hand was some comfort. She could hear her own breath sobbing in her throat. The car was better protection than nothing, although high velocity bullets could go straight through the metal panels and explode in soft human flesh. Such deadly projectiles would only be stopped by the bulkiest of vests — kevlar with ceramic plates — but they were both wearing the lighter version. And nothing could protect their heads . . .

BODY GUARD

A DETECTIVE INSPECTOR CAROL ASHTON MYSTERY

BY
CLAIRE McNAB

THE NAIAD PRESS
1995

Printed in the United States of America on acid-free paper
First Edition
First printing November, 1994
Second printing February, 1995

Edited by Katherine V. Forrest
Cover design by Bonnie Liss (Phoenix Graphics)
Typeset by Sandi Stancil

Library of Congress Cataloging-in-Publication Data

McNab, Claire.
    Body guard / Claire McNab.
        p.   cm.
    ISBN 1-56280-073-6
    I. Title.
PS3563.C3877B63   1994
813'.54—dc20

94-15981
CIP

For Sheila

Acknowledgments

Special mention to Lyn and to Marion for specialized information regarding Brisbane, the friendliest of cities.

And to the best of editors, Katherine Forrest, my thanks.

About the Author

Claire McNab is the author of the Detective Inspector Carol Ashton mysteries, *Lessons in Murder, Fatal Reunion, Death Down Under, Cop Out, Dead Certain* and *Body Guard*. She has also written two romances, *Under the Southern Cross* and *Silent Heart*. While a high school English teacher she began her writing career with comedy plays and textbooks. After she became a full-time writer she wrote for television soap opera. In her native Australia she is known for her self-help and children's books.

For reasons of the heart, Claire is now a permanent resident of the United States. She lives in Los Angeles, which she says is, "Exciting — but absolutely nothing like Sydney!"

PROLOGUE

The mail room was humming with conversation as letters were opened and consigned to baskets according to category: standard reply; non-standard reply; requiring Marla Strickland's personal attention; requests for appearances; donations; financial records and accounts; hate mail.

"Hey, Esther, those are great stamps. Save them for my kid, will you?"

Esther Duncan sighed with irritation as she tried to open the heavily sealed padded envelope. Finally she grabbed a pair of scissors and cut across one end.

There was a flash of light and a flat clap of raw sound. Then the smell of smoke and burned flesh.

Marla Strickland came striding out of her office.

"What the hell . . . ?" She stopped, appalled.

Somebody whimpered. The woman kneeling beside the sprawled body looked up, blanched with shock. "She's dead. Esther's dead."

Marla had a confused thought that Esther Duncan was now better off dead than alive — the explosion had blown away most of her face.

CHAPTER ONE

Detective Inspector Carol Ashton slid carefully out of the chair and moved to look out of the window. How odd to be in the Commissioner's office dressed informally in jeans and a shirt. She suppressed a wince as the now familiar pain flared deep in her right side.

The buildings of the city of Sydney glowed in the clear summer light and the water of the harbor behind them was so blue it looked painted. "I don't want to do it," she said. She changed focus, seeing her face reflected in the glass — hollow-cheeked, straight blonde hair much shorter than her customary style. As soon as she'd got out of hospital she'd had it cut.

The Commissioner's sleek leather chair creaked under his weight as he leaned back. "I know you're not fully fit to return to active duty ..."

"It's not that." She turned to face him. "I want to get back to work as soon as possible."

"So what's your problem? Marla Strickland or the role of bodyguard?"

Carol surveyed the hulking man who had been her mentor for much of her career. "Both."

His expression remained implacable. "That's too bad, Carol. You're the one."

She threw her hands up impatiently. "Why isn't it ASIO's baby? The letter bomb was posted from Australia, so it's a matter of international terrorism, isn't it? As far as I'm concerned, Australian security can have it." She thought wryly that it was ironic to find herself assigning any job to the Australian Security Intelligence Organization — it was more usual that both state and federal police fought ASIO over areas of responsibility.

"ASIO *is* involved. *And* the FBI, not to mention the CIA. It's a political decision to appoint you to protect the woman." He sighed irritably. "Look, Carol, I'm not happy about it either. I pointed out that any bodyguard with a high media profile like yours is hamstrung from the word go, but that didn't cut any ice."

"Hasn't Marla Strickland got her own security?"

He flicked open the embossed folder on his desk. "Her head office in Connecticut supplied more information than I ever intended to know. And because of the quantity of mail threats she gets, there's plenty of background stuff from the FBI as well. Apparently when she tours in the States she hires armed guards at every venue. Her speech last March when she announced that God hated women stirred up so much controversy that she was forced to screen audiences with metal detectors. But as far as her organization's concerned, she's only got one security officer — who doubles as Strickland's assistant — and no personal bodyguard."

He watched as Carol left the window to return to her chair. "It may not be much consolation, but Marla Strickland is fighting your appointment as much as you are." He smiled cynically. "However, we can't afford to have America's — if not the world's — most famous feminist killed or injured while in Australia. Apart from anything else, it might put a dent in tourism."

"There's any number of perfectly adequate security officers —"

"This isn't a matter for argument, Carol. I'm telling you, not asking you. Strickland flies in on Wednesday, and I expect you to meet her." He raised a hand before Carol could respond. "I know the international airport is Federal Police jurisdiction. You're there for PR, nothing else."

She frowned at his tone. "And if I refuse?"

He heaved his bulk out of the leather chair. "Are you considering promotion? Chief Inspector Carol Ashton sounds good to me."

She gave an incredulous laugh. "If the stick doesn't work on me, you'll try the carrot?"

He looked at her gravely. "Carol, I have pressure too. I told you it's a political decision to appoint you.

Don't ask me why, because I don't know the answer. I've suggested other people; I've said you're not fully fit . . ." He shrugged his heavy shoulders. "It seems you're the one."

"Great."

Her obvious disgust earned a slight smile. "There are plenty of people who'd do a great deal to even meet the famous Marla Strickland."

"I'm not one of them," said Carol.

Detective Sergeant Mark Bourke was delighted to see her. His homely, comfortable face split with a grin, he opened the door of her office and took from her arms the pile of files the Commissioner had given her. "Welcome back, Carol!"

"I'm not exactly back."

He made a face. "So the rumor you're to be bodyguard to a star is true?"

"Some star."

Bourke ran a hand over his short brown hair which had recently begun to recede at the temples. "I heard it was Marla Strickland, feminist extraordinaire."

She felt tired and depressed. "Rumor, unfortunately, is right."

He looked as disgusted as she felt. "And all because some loony in Australia airmailed her a letter bomb."

"She certainly makes a lot of enemies, although what she's done to annoy someone in Tasmania I don't know."

"Pat thinks Strickland's okay because she's

presiding at an opening of an exhibition of Australian women artists at her Art Gallery." Bourke hadn't been married long, and his voice softened when he mentioned his wife's name. "Maybe she'll be a sweetheart in person."

"From all accounts I doubt it." She cleared a corner for him to put down the armful of dossiers concerning the feminist's tour. "Look, Mark, the Commissioner told me it's a political decision to appoint me official bodyguard, but it was obvious he wouldn't, or couldn't, tell me any more than that. Do me a favor — ask around. You've got contacts in the most amazing places. I'd like to know why I've been landed with this job, considering it needs a specialist in the area of martial arts and personal protection, and I'm not one."

"Okay, but it'll take a while ... if I can get anything at all."

She sighed at the sight of her desk covered with reports and memos. The in-tray was overflowing. Somehow she'd thought that Bourke would achieve the same neatness with her work as both his person and his own desk always showed. She looked at him accusingly. "I thought you were looking after the paperwork for me."

"I have been. You should have seen it before I got to work. The only stuff left is for your personal attention." He laughed at her expression. "Well, each memo says urgent at the top ..."

As she slumped into her well-worn chair, his expression changed to one of concern. "Carol, are you all right?"

"I'm fine."

His jaw tightened. "If I'd been quicker —"

7

"It wouldn't have made any difference."

It had seemed a simple arrest of a nineteen-year-old boy who had lost his temper and fatally struck his father with a tire iron, then tried to set it up as a burglary gone wrong. Carol wouldn't have been there, except that she'd felt sorry for the kid. She'd imagined her own son, now eleven, as a troubled teenager like the wide-eyed young man who'd cried during his interview, then reddened with embarrassment at the raw emotion he'd showed. With no eyewitnesses and awaiting confirmatory forensic evidence, they'd let him go back to his shattered mother, who had no idea her son might be a suspect in her husband's death.

That warm spring day in early September, when Mark Bourke had put his head into her office to say the father's blood splatters on the son's clothes tied him to the murder, Carol, entirely on impulse, decided to go with Bourke for the arrest. There'd been no suggestion that the suspect would present any danger, no warning that he'd stolen a friend's hunting rifle. Carol and Bourke had parked in front of the modest house, walked up the path, their weapons holstered, presenting no obvious threat — other than perhaps a revealing grimness of expression.

The scene was still vivid in Carol's imagination: the bedraggled hydrangea bushes lining the path, the tired plants in plastic pots on the veranda, the front door that needed a coat of paint. The sound of the door chime — an incongruous deep-toned carillon. The mother opening the door, the son behind in the hallway screaming for her to get out of the way, the gleam of light on metal...

Mark Bourke lunging forward, the flash from the barrel seeming to be simultaneous with the jolt of the bullet as it struck. And the disbelief flooding Carol as she fell, all her mobility and strength blown away in a splinter of time.

The physical pain of being shot had been wrenching, but the ache over Sybil had been worse. At least, Carol thought caustically, Sybil had waited until she had nearly recovered from her injury before announcing that she was taking a course in women's studies in London that would mean she would be away from Australia for a year.

Carol could recall the smell of breakfast toast in the kitchen, the raucous cry of a cockatoo in a eucalyptus gum tree overhanging the deck outside, the sunlight slanting through the glass doors to turn Sybil's red hair to flame. "I know this will sound trite," Sybil had said, "but I'm not willing to put everything into our relationship when you just coast along ignoring any problems. We never talk, you won't give anything of yourself, concede any need. We aren't going anywhere, Carol — or anywhere I want to go."

Furious, Carol had snapped, "I love you. Isn't that enough?"

Sybil shook her had slowly. "No. It isn't. It was once. Not anymore."

"I won't beg."

Sybil had smiled, even though her hazel eyes were brimming. "I never thought you would."

Resentful anger had thickened Carol's voice. "Your timing is wonderful, darling. I imagine I should be grateful you waited until I was out of the hospital."

"Carol, even when you were wounded you didn't

need me. You closed yourself off and pretended you hadn't nearly died. You're the dearest person on earth to me, but I just can't live with you. Not the way it is now." She paused. "Maybe things will change when we're apart and have a different perspective."

Carol's bitterness was acid on her tongue. "Leaving your options open, are you? Don't count on me to still be here if you change your mind."

Sybil's expression had been unreadable. "I won't."

Bourke's voice broke into her thoughts. "Carol?" She looked up to meet his concerned gaze. "You shouldn't be here. You're not well enough yet."

"I'm fine."

Her flat tone didn't dissuade him. "You can't be on call twenty-four hours a day, especially when you're touring with Strickland. You're not up to it."

She took a deep breath. There was no reason to be angry with Mark. Besides being a valuable colleague with whom she'd worked for years, he was a personal friend who'd totally supported her when she'd come out of the closet, her reluctant admission that she was a lesbian having been forced on her by a blackmail attempt during a high-profile case. "Don't worry, Mark, I'm not a masochist. The Commissioner's agreed to let me take Anne Newsome with me as back-up."

He frowned. "Anne's working with me at the moment and we've got quite a caseload."

Carol felt both irritated and guilty. She knew the extra load Mark had carried during her absence, and now she was taking someone from him. None of this showed in her cool voice. "I'm sorry, Mark, but that's the way it is."

His frown vanished as he touched her lightly on the shoulder. "Great to have you back, even if you *are* just passing through."

She stretched her arms above her head, ignoring for a moment the pain that stabbed her side. "You won't be so cheerful when I tell you that anything on my desk I can't deal with today goes right back to you."

His smile disappeared. "Bloody hell!"

CHAPTER TWO

"Heavens," said Detective Anne Newsome, her voice almost drowned by the sustained rumble of excited conversations.

Surveying the crush of mainly female supporters of Marla Strickland, Carol smiled at her companion's mild exclamation. On this, a weekday mid-afternoon, the arrival area of Sydney International Airport was crammed with a crowd that overflowed into the roadway, swamping the usual people who had come to meet friends and relatives. Though most of the crowd seemed to be Marla Strickland enthusiasts, through the cacophony the thin voices of a small group of Family First followers could be faintly heard chanting anti-feminist slogans. Both the media and Federal police moved forward when MARLA STRICKLAND KILLS BABIES was torn from Family First hands and trampled by a couple of furious Strickland supporters.

"Detective Inspector Ashton?" Tall, fair-haired, a smile crinkling his vivid blue eyes, the man reached inside his rather crumpled gray suit to flash his identification as a Federal Police officer. When Carol moved to return the gesture he grinned. "No need. Since you're on television every second day I know what you look like." He looked at Anne. "Detective Newsome? I'm Sid Safer — and don't bother to make any cracks about my name."

Anne Newsome smiled up at him. "Want to see my identification?"

"Nah. Her say-so's as good as gold." His nod indicated Carol. "Come on, you two. You're late. Plane's been down for half an hour and Marla Strickland's putting on a performance."

He led them through a series of security doors, each guarded by an officer. "If it was up to me, I'd be inclined to let them do her in," he said good-humoredly as he ushered them through a final door.

Carol could hear an American voice raised in ire. "I don't give a goddamn *shit* about security! Those women out there have waited for hours to see me!"

Sid Safer nodded to a fellow officer on the door and neatly inserted Carol, Ann and himself into the celebrity lounge. A slight young man with a wispy mustache who'd been leaning in the doorway, arms folded, moved out of the way. From briefing papers Carol recognized him as the feminist's stepson, Gary Hawkins. Apart from him, Marla Strickland was traveling with only two other staff, Pam Boyle, a PR liaison, and Strickland's principal assistant, Beverly Diaz.

"Ms. Strickland, you'll be pleased to meet your own personal bodyguard." Safer's voice resonated with hearty irony. "This is Detective Inspector Carol Ashton."

The woman who swung around was familiar from her photographs — shoulder-length dark hair, a thin, intelligent face with patrician bone structure, finely arched eyebrows, a wide mouth — but there was a vitality that no flat picture could catch. Dressed in a beautifully cut navy blue suit with a frothy white blouse, she looked very feminine, and very tough. When she spoke, her voice had a taut certainty. "I've been told all about you, Inspector, but I don't want, or need, a bodyguard."

"My sentiments exactly."

Marla Strickland's grin was ferocious. "Then why are you here?"

"I had an offer I couldn't refuse."

"And her?"

Carol's eyes narrowed at the woman's imperious tone. "Detective Anne Newsome. She's back-up as I can't be awake twenty-four hours a day."

"No? They tell me you're superhuman, Inspector."

"They may. I won't."

Marla looked at the young detective critically. "She's very young."

Anne Newsome amused Carol by saying calmly,

"I've been fully trained in anti-terrorism and I'm an excellent shot. I hope that reassures you, Ms. Strickland."

"I've been told Australia's very safe — no handguns, right? So I don't need any reassurance. I'm not in any danger."

An Airport Security officer with a sharp Dick Tracy profile interposed, "I was just explaining to Ms. Strickland that for safety reasons she couldn't leave the airport by way of the front entrance..." He looked hopefully at Carol, obviously banking on her support. "We have a car waiting on the tarmac to take her to another exit."

"And I, Inspector, was explaining how I can't ignore anyone who's come to meet me, whether they're for or against me."

Carol was conscious that Sid Safer was grinning in the background. She wiped the smile off his face by saying, "Then we'll move your transport to the front of the terminal. It'll take a short time to get everyone into position — say twenty minutes — and then we'll leave."

Her announcement seemed to upset the young man who'd been holding up the wall smoothing his embryonic mustache. He straightened with a grunt, and left the room.

The American didn't seem pleased either. "Just like that? Aren't you worried about my safety?"

"Of course, but I presume you won't change your mind —"

"You've got *that* right!" Marla Strickland appraised the understated elegance of Carol's gray suit. "You don't look like a dyke."

15

Carol smiled briefly. "Neither do you."

That brought the woman's chin up. "I'm *married,* Inspector."

"So was I."

An extremely tall woman with an undisciplined mane of frizzy brown hair slipped through the door, trying, Carol thought, to look as unobtrusive as possible but only making herself stand out all the more. "Marla? There are protesters waiting. You shouldn't insist —"

"Pam, this is Detective Inspector Ashton. *She* doesn't mind if I go out the front way. Inspector, this is Pam Boyle."

Pam Boyle's height seemed to embarrass her. She ducked her head and averted her gaze. This stiff, awkward woman, Carol knew, was a direct marketing expert who'd been poached from a multi-national company to work at promoting Marla Strickland. Carol shook hands, although Pam Boyle snatched hers back as quickly as possible. "Ms. Boyle? May I introduce my colleague, Detective Anne Newsome."

The tall woman darted a glance at Anne. "But there's only supposed to be one bodyguard . . ."

"Inspector Ashton needs her rest, Pam. She's just recovered from a gunshot wound." Marla smiled triumphantly at Carol. "I researched everyone in detail."

"Then perhaps you have some idea who wants to kill you."

A snort of derision. "Plenty of people *think* about killing me — but as for doing it . . ." She shrugged elaborately. "That letter bomb wasn't meant for me personally. It was sent by some inadequate Australian male who couldn't get it up and wanted to make an explosive statement instead."

"A member of your staff died," said Carol coldly, "and the device could have taken out others if they'd been closer, including you."

Marla Strickland stared soberly at Carol, then gestured irritably at herself. "I'm putting up with the discomfort of a bullet-proof vest now, if that's any consolation."

"It isn't if they go for a head shot," said Carol. She eyed the woman's trim figure. "And judging from the lack of bulk it must be a lightweight vest, so you won't have full protection from a high-velocity bullet."

"Then as my bodyguard I presume you'll be prepared to throw yourself in front of me," Marla Strickland said tartly.

"Your best bet is to drop to the floor. If I tell you to, *do* it. Don't stop to ask questions."

In the arrival hall the numbers of spectators had been swelled by yet another television crew, which was trolling the crowd for useful sound bites. Sid Safer nodded to Carol. "Everyone's in position, but you know in a situation like this we haven't got much control."

Carol checked out the setup. Federal officers stood with their backs to the door through which Marla Strickland would enter the hall, ready to form a wedge to force a way through the crowd. Others were stationed throughout the hall, alert for any hostile act. "Maybe someone will put us out of a job," said Carol with a slight smile.

Safer's amused reply was drowned by a roar from

the crowd as Marla Strickland appeared. She raised her arms in her characteristic clenched-hands gesture. Her abrasive voice rose above the hubbub: "A great hello to a great country!" Another roar of approval.

"Oh, please!" said Anne close to Carol's ear. "I've seen her on television often enough . . . She says that everywhere she goes." She added, "It works every time."

Surrounded by security, with Carol close behind her, Marla Strickland was hustled through the press to the first of two stretch limousines — the second was for her staff. Protected from eager eyes by the heavily tinted glass, she sank back into the black leather seats with a sigh, her face flushed. She turned to Carol beside her in the back seat. "This is going to be a wonderful tour — I feel it already! Tell me about Family First. I liked the way they were screaming at me. It's the contrast . . . it makes everything better."

Sid Safer and Anne Newsome, seated across from them in the backward-facing limousine seats, exchanged glances. Safer stretched out his long legs. "Your staff was given briefing papers on any group or organization that might oppose your tour. Haven't you read them?"

Marla Strickland's displeasure was clear. "I don't have time to read every bureaucratic memo." Frowning, she glanced at the back of the driver's head. "And I particularly asked that *women* be assigned to my entourage."

"Come on," said Safer, "*you've* got a male on your staff."

"Gary is my stepson," Marla snapped. "He handles the transport logistics."

Safer spread his hands. "Well, that's all right, then."

Frowning at his mocking tone, she said, "Isn't there a woman at your rank available?"

Safer grinned. "Probably, but I don't imagine anyone in the Feds took your suggestion seriously." He glanced at Carol. "The State cops seem to have taken you more to heart, or you wouldn't have Inspector Ashton."

"Ms. Strickland's objecting to me, too," said Carol mildly.

Safer's smile widened. "There's no pleasing some people."

The American's mouth gave an irritated twitch, but otherwise she chose to ignore his comment. Turning to Carol she said, "I suppose Family First is a right-wing fundamentalist group? I noticed anti-abortion placards."

"I'm sure they'd prefer the term pro-life." Carol added, "Family First is heavily into traditional values."

"Traditional values?" Marla sneered. "You mean patriarchy gone mad, where women are where men want them — the bedroom or the kitchen — silenced and isolated. And the mere wave of the Bible to justify it."

"Lunatic fringe," said Safer. It wasn't clear whether he was referring to Family First or Marla Strickland. "But it's a free country."

His comment was not well received. "Free? Australia's defamation laws are off the wall! I'm told I can't directly name the men and organizations who keep women down, because if I do I'll be slapped with a libel suit!"

19

"You sure can't carry on the way you usually do."
When she glared at Safer, he put up his hands. "I
always read my briefing papers and watch my
briefing videotapes. I'm very familiar with your
modus operandi."

His sardonic tone didn't have the effect Carol
expected. Marla Strickland's face relaxed into a smile
that was unexpectedly charming. Carol couldn't
remember a photograph where she'd looked so
pleasant. Marla said, "You remind me a little of my
husband."

Safer looked astonished. "I do?"

"He's not as attractive as you are — but he can
be just as opinionated."

While Safer digested this, Anne Newsome said,
"Does your husband ever come on tours with you?"

"Roy can't spare the time. He's a pediatrician
with an extremely busy practice."

The glass window separating the driver from the
passengers slid down. "We're at the back entrance of
the hotel. Cleever's here."

Safer stretched forward to open the door. "I can
hardly wait . . ."

Before he could touch the handle the door was
opened by a woman with severely cut honey-blonde
hair. Wearing jeans, a loose pink top and sneakers,
she bent down to look into the limo. "Ms. Strickland,
Inspector Ashton, Detective Newsome . . ." Her long
mouth curled in a slight smile. "And Safer."

As Safer clambered out of the car, Marla
Strickland said to Carol, "Who's she?"

Carol had spent several hours of briefing sessions
with the agent. "Denise Cleever. She's with ASIO."

"That's the same as our CIA, isn't it?"

"Yes. ASIO looks after Australia's internal security. They're involved because the letter bomb sent to your office originated in Australia."

Marla stepped out of the vehicle. Above her towered the angled glass walls of the hotel. Hands on hips, she planted herself in front of Denise Cleever. "Haven't you been told? My company, Strickland Enterprises, has a contract with a private security firm. You won't be needed."

"We've checked out your security company, Ms. Strickland —"

"That's already been done from the States! The firm's entirely reputable. I've spoken to its principal, Cynthia Huntling, myself."

"I agree. Huntling Security itself checks out. We were interested in individual employees."

"Waste of time. I presume you found nothing."

Denise Cleever nodded agreeably. "Nothing."

"And they're in place?"

"Two Huntling Security guards are waiting for you in the penthouse suite."

"Then I see no reason for you to be here." Marla gestured towards Carol. "As you see, I have Inspector Ashton with me as a personal bodyguard."

The agent's expression was impassive. "My orders are to stay with you until further notice."

Safer put out his hand. "But for the meantime, *I* can say goodbye, Ms. Strickland."

She ignored his hand, gestured peremptorily at the small gaggle of her staff that had emerged from the second limo and then strode off towards the back entrance of the luxury hotel.

"Well, Carol," said Denise Cleever with a grin, "that sure is one charming lady."

* * * * *

It was dark when Carol pulled into the carport above her house. She wished it had been earlier, so she could have gone out to the broad deck that ran the length of the place. She needed the soothing view of Middle Harbour surrounded by thickly wooded slopes of eucalyptus gums, the chatter of rainbow lorikeets in the branches above, the peace that watching the sun set always gave her.

As Carol wearily opened her front door, her Aunt Sarah called out from the back of the house. "Carol? I've kept something hot for you. I know you won't have eaten."

She was grateful that Aunt Sarah, her closest, best-loved relative, had volunteered to come down from her mountain home at Leura and stay while Carol traipsed around Australia with Marla Strickland's tour. The house echoed emptily now that Sybil was gone and even the close feline attentions of Sinker and Jeffrey had been unable to lessen her loneliness.

Her aunt, white hair haloing her tanned face, smiled at her with green eyes very like her own. She was sitting cross-legged on the couch, wearing a cerise jumpsuit with startling yellow flowers appliqued across the front and down one leg. Jeffrey's fat ginger body, curled purring in her lap, provided another jolting color clash. Aunt Sarah patted the flowers on her plump chest. "Like it? I did it myself."

"It's different, Aunt Sarah, but then — so are you."

Sinker's black and white form came stalking across the polished floor, his tail snapping with impatience. "Carol, he's been fed. Don't let him fool you."

Carol slid onto one of the tall stools at the breakfast bench. "I'm so tired, anyone could fool me at the moment."

Removing a protesting Jeffrey, Aunt Sarah got up and bustled into the kitchen. "Food and a good night's sleep is what you need."

A few minutes later, Carol yawned over a helping of her aunt's special steak and kidney pie. "Any mail?"

Her aunt handed her a postcard. "This is from David — he's enjoying Bali. He'll be back in a week or two, won't he?"

Carol smiled at the mention of David's name. "More like two weeks. Justin and Eleanor want to explore the island outside the usual tourist areas." Her ex-husband had custody of their eleven-year-old son, although Carol saw him every weekend.

David's scrawled message on the reverse of the garish postcard made her ache to see him. "He's learned how to scuba dive." She could hear the pride in her voice.

The last line he'd written was: *I love you, Mum.* Carol ran her fingertips over the words. In the hospital, when she'd been in intensive care, her surgeon had allowed David to see her for a few minutes. Sybil had held David's hand tightly as he approached the bed where Carol lay in the grip of a fatigue so absolute that the mere effort of breathing was exhausting. She could still remember his wide-eyed, white face and the desperation in his voice when he had whispered, "You aren't going to die, Mum, are you?"

She had struggled to smile, to reassure him that she would always be there for him, but his eyes had filled with tears as he had touched her hand. "Please don't die, Mum. Please."

Carol felt her own eyes tear up at the memory. She blinked rapidly, then, conscious that her aunt was watching her, said brusquely, "Any other mail?"

"Just bills . . . and something from Sybil."

Shoving the envelope from Sybil to one side, Carol said, "I'll look at it later."

"What went wrong, darling?"

"Sybil didn't discuss it with you? I thought she would."

Her aunt's rough-textured, work-worn hand cupped Carol's chin. "She didn't say anything. Just that she loved you."

Carol twisted away. "I'd like some coffee. Can I get you some?"

"Don't you move. I'll do it." As she busied herself with Carol's ancient percolator, she said, "Forgot to tell you, but Madeline Shipley phoned. Wants you to get back to her when you can."

Ignoring the shiver of response at the name, Carol said off-handedly, "I'll call her tomorrow."

"Caught her TV show this evening." Aunt Sarah sniffed. "Usual sensational stuff. And the promos were for a special she's doing on the Strickland tour, so she probably wants to milk you for any info you've got."

"Then Madeline will be disappointed. I don't know any more than she does."

"Marla Strickland's media conference will be on the late news." Aunt Sarah turned on the small television on the counter top. "Were you there?"

Carol wriggled her shoulders to release some of the tension. "Yes, but you won't see me. I kept out of camera range."

"Unusual for you." Her aunt grinned.

The media had set up microphones and cameras in the hotel conference room, and the American feminist had emerged after a shower and change of clothing with her smooth public persona firmly in place. The television news segment gave Carol a much better viewpoint than she'd had at the time. She'd been behind a screen placed so that she could watch Marla Strickland from a side angle, but not be seen herself.

Carol had to admit the woman had presented a charming, but decisive image. She'd shown an excellent knowledge of local politics and the principal women's groups, and had even made a few mild jokes to gain accepting laughter from the media representatives.

"What's she really like?" asked Aunt Sarah.

"Over the top."

"I don't agree with everything she says, but we need women like her."

Carol had to smile at her aunt's emphatic tone. "We do? She alienates more people than she convinces." She glanced at the untidy pile of books on the coffee table. Marla Strickland's titles had been supplied to her as background: *Fundamentalists Despise Women . . . Yes They Do; Vagina Envy and Religious Theory.* There was a hardback advance copy of the latest book to be launched during the

Australian tour: *God Hates Women: De-sexing the Patriarchal Deity*. "Have you had a chance to look through her books?"

Aunt Sarah tut-tutted. "Carol, I have my *own* copies. Besides that, as I'm the president of the Blue Mountains Women's Discussion Group, we've had some wonderful arguments over the points Marla Strickland raises. The only one I haven't seen before is this one." She picked up the hardback and handed it to Carol. "Have you read it?"

On the front cover a red circle with a slash through it was superimposed over the conventional image of God as a bearded old man in flowing robes. The back jacket had a color photo of the author staring arrogantly at the camera. "Not really. I haven't had time."

Her aunt grinned. "Even if you had days to fill, you wouldn't read it, would you?"

"No. I can't stand being preached at."

"I prefer to think Marla Strickland proselytizes."

"A long word doesn't change things," Carol laughed, "it's still brainwashing."

CHAPTER THREE

Its mellow sandstone walls floodlit, the Sydney Town Hall, an ornate Victorian structure with an elaborate clock tower, refused to be cowed by looming office buildings or by the magnificence of the Queen Victoria Building squatting to the north on an entire city block. The wide shallow steps at the Town Hall main entrance provided seats for many people enjoying the evening air, while other people streamed past and into a marble-floored vestibule dominated by a richly glittering crystal chandelier. On the footpath outside, the television cameras had been attracted by a group of grim-faced Family First supporters holding placards denouncing Marla Strickland. THE VOICE OF EVIL HAS A HONEYED TONGUE was one that had amused the crowd and occasioned several ribald comments.

"We're keeping an eye on them," said Denise Cleever to Carol as they stood observing the entry, "although I don't think they're into letter bombs."

"How close an eye?"

Denise was wearing anonymous casual clothes and a loose top. She grinned as she patted her waist where Carol knew she had a gun concealed. "They'd be so flattered if they knew we're treating them as though they're urban terrorists. The truth is, Family First has quite a sophisticated system going, with a network of believers ready to contact every influential public figure by using the full range of electronic and personal communications as well as a barrage of letters to the media. Apart from that, the only violence members have been involved with is when they've been attacked by people who overreact to Family First's conservative views."

"What about the abortion clinic bombing last year? Family First had a picket line there."

"And they got a lot of positive publicity by expressing shock, horror and indignation. Besides, you cops couldn't come up with any link between them and the bomb, could you?"

"No, but I've always been wary of anyone to the far right of Hitler."

Denise raised her eyebrows. "I never would have picked you for a left-wing trendy."

Carol grinned. "I'm not. I think I'm determinedly center of the road."

"Not so center. It took guts to come out of the closet when you're a cop. It's not a profession noted for its broadmindedness."

Carol shrugged. "Coming out was more an accident than anything else." She thought bitterly of the circumstances that had forced her to reveal her sexual orientation. Sybil had been so impatient with her angry resentment, so pleased, as she put it, that it was "no longer an issue." But, of course, it was. Used to having a degree of control in most situations, this was one where she had no power to orchestrate events or even anticipate when her lesbianism might be a problem.

Her appointment as bodyguard for Marla Strickland was a case in point: the American hadn't been tactful when they had been alone in the penthouse suite. "Look, Inspector —"

"Please call me Carol. I intend to call you Marla."

"Okay, Carol, let me lay it on the line. I can't afford to have a known lesbian closely associated with me. It's not a matter of prejudice, of course."

"I'm sure some of your best friends are lesbians," said Carol dryly.

Marla made an impatient gesture. "It's a matter of politics."

Carol folded her arms. "I would have thought lesbian women would support you over rights for women in general."

"They do, and I appreciate that very much. As I said, it's politics. It's so easy for people who oppose me — and don't think for one moment they aren't ruthless and powerful — to beat me with the lesbian stick. Do you know what I mean?"

"Not really."

Marla sighed. "If they can say I'm a man-hating dyke, or that I associate closely with man-hating dykes, then they can blunt my influence, persuade all those ordinary women living ordinary lives that I'm a dangerous radical."

"Aren't you?"

Amused, Marla chuckled. "Well, yes, Carol — I am. But it won't help my cause if I frighten off middle-America, or, for that matter, middle-Australia. God knows, the word feminist is enough of a burden to carry with those women."

"You're stuck with me, Marla. I've tried to get out of this assignment as hard as you've tried to get rid of me, but it's no go."

"It's nothing personal, but I'm not giving up."

Carol's smile had been sour. "I hope you succeed."

A bellow of sound brought her back to the present. A man, polished boyish smile in place, was alighting from an official car. "The Minister for Knitting," said Denise unkindly. Joseph Marin, the Federal Minister for Cultural Affairs, paused on the Town Hall steps to smile broadly into television cameras. "He's such a wanker. Have you met him?"

Carol nodded. "Several times. He likes to spread himself around."

"You're telling me! And he's got serious delusions of grandeur. Not only does he think he's prime minister material, he's always imagining he's the target of some terrorist group, so he's constantly asking for ASIO briefings about perceived threats. The thing is, no self-respecting terrorist would be seen dead killing him." They watched the minister disappear inside after a final wave to the crowd. "Speaking of killing, who's guarding Strickland?"

"Anne Newsome. I'll take over as soon as she comes out to speak."

"Newsome any good? She seems awfully young."

Carol grinned ruefully. "You're suggesting when the cops start looking young, it means you're getting old?"

The ASIO agent eyed her appreciatively. "*You* still look pretty sensational."

Surprised at the warmth of the compliment, Carol said, "Thanks . . ."

Catching her sideways look, Denise smiled. "I'm a sister, Carol."

"Really?"

"Really. Security clearance at ASIO doesn't require you to be heterosexual, just to be out and comfortable with your sexuality, so you can't be blackmailed."

"It doesn't make any difference to me, one way or the other." Carol's tone was dismissive.

Denise's smile broadened. "Well it sure as hell makes a difference to me."

The hum of the waiting audience, electric with anticipation, eased every time someone walked onto the stage, then resumed when it was obvious it wasn't Marla Strickland making her entrance. The stage jutted out into the auditorium and Carol stood beside it looking up at the packed balconies that ran on three sides of the main hall. "This is a security nightmare," she said to Anne Newsome. "Have you checked whether the Huntling Security people are patrolling the top floor corridors?"

31

"They're in place, though I don't know how much good they'll be if anything happens."

"While she's speaking I want you on the left side of the stage. If there's an attack, the lectern's been bullet-proofed with kevlar, so get her down behind it. You've got your vest on?"

"Yes, and so has Marla Strickland, though she protested. She said it spoiled the line of her outfit."

Carol spoke into the tiny microphone attached to her jacket lapel. "Ten minutes, everyone." She tapped Anne's arm. "Okay, get familiar with your location and note any danger spots. And remember, don't watch La Strickland enter — watch the people watching her."

Carol waited while Anne got into position. After an initial wariness, she'd come to appreciate the young constable's abilities. Her average appearance — curly gold-brown hair, dark eyes and olive skin — concealed acute intelligence and keen ambition. Under Mark Bourke's guidance she was developing outstanding investigative skills.

As Carol approached the dressing room she could hear Marla Strickland's raised voice. "I don't care if threats have been called in from every state in Australia! It's enough I have to put up with a bodyguard *and* an ASIO officer. I've got my own security and I don't need anything else."

A woman said something soothing, then Sid Safer's attempt at a conciliatory tone made Carol's lips twitch. "Ms. Strickland, I understand how upsetting this can be —"

"The only thing upsetting me is *you*."

As Carol entered the room, Sid raised one eyebrow to her, then continued in a voice of sweet reason, "Surely you find the death threat faxed to your hotel, plus several unpleasant phone calls, disturbing, if nothing else. I'd think you'd want *more* security, not less."

Marla inspected her coral-tipped fingernails. "I'm used to threats. One in a million intends to carry it out."

Not intending to buy into the argument, Carol helped herself to a cup of coffee. She nodded to Pam Boyle, who had twisted her long frame into a chair in the corner of the room and was vainly attempting to smooth her frizzy hair with the palms of her hands.

The other woman standing by Marla was more interesting. Her photograph in Carol's briefing folder had shown her steel-gray hair, her dark eyes and cupid's bow mouth, but not the concentrated black stare she used like a laser, nor the rigidity of her posture. Beverly Diaz stood at attention beside her leader as though on a parade ground. She studied Carol efficiently, her gaze as unemotional as if she were a machine.

"We haven't met." Carol extended a hand. "I'm Carol Ashton."

"I know who you are." Her voice was soft, but intense. She touched palms in the briefest of handshakes without mentioning her own name.

Marla put an arm around the woman's stiff shoulders. "Carol, this is my right-hand woman. I couldn't do without Bev. She's my personal assistant, and . . ." Marla shot a look at Safer, ". . . Bev deals with all security matters, so I'm in safe hands."

"You've had training?" said Safer. "It isn't in your CV."

33

Beverly's black stare didn't waver. "Then your records are at fault."

A short, worried man was allowed in by the guard on the door. "Excuse me, Ms. Strickland, but the dignitaries are all seated and we *are* running a little late..." He smiled deferentially as he tapped his watch. "If you wouldn't mind..."

"Bev, my notes. Pam, it's time you went to the back of the hall. Find Gary and take him with you."

Safer looked curious as Pam Boyle uncurled her length and hurried out of the room. "Back of the hall? What's that for?"

Marla was making a last check of her makeup. "Pam's job is to assess reactions to the points I raise. If I need to fine-tune my presentation I want details of what works and what doesn't. Up on the stage, with the lights on me, I could miss some of the subtleties of audience response." She smoothed an eyebrow, then turned to Carol. "Ready to put your life on the line, Inspector?" Without waiting for an answer she said to the short man, "One minute and I'll be on stage. Make sure the Mayor's ready to introduce me..."

At her entry, Marla raised her arms in salute as she was greeted with a roar of acclamation, then she waited passively at the lectern for silence. She allowed the quietness to last for a long moment, then said deliberately, "You have heard that I have said that God hates women. You may have thought that an exaggeration." She paused. "It is truer than you can imagine. Up there..." Marla gestured heavenward, "... lives the patriarchal God our society has worshipped in blind obedience to the commands of a male hierarchy." Her voice had risen in volume and conviction. "That God is unambiguously male and is personified as a loving father. Some father! A heavenly parent who would condemn the female half of the population to servitude and powerlessness. A celestial parent who ratifies the actions of the spiritual, psychological, cultural and *physical* bullies who can only find personal identity by glorying in the accident of birth that gave them maleness." She leaned forward, her hands on either side of the lectern. "And the pity is, some women support them in this!"

Carol was concentrated on any movement around the stage, so she only glanced at Marla from time to time, but videotapes she'd watched as part of her briefing had already given her some impression of the drama and force of the woman's stage presence. Marla used her voice superbly, varying volume, speed, and intonation to create a mesmerizing performance. "The population of the United States is two hundred and fifty million," said Marla conversationally. "Almost a quarter claim to accept the warped fundamentalist view of the universe. Millions more support the anti-woman cant of extremists in the major religions, including Roman Catholic and Muslim." She raised one hand. "It is *their* God who hates women!"

The glare of floodlights emphasized Marla Strickland's dark hair and pale, thin face. Her wide eyes glowed with the truth of her words. And she knew the value of silence: she spoke in short, graceful sentences, her voice rising to emphasize the

35

point, and then she paused, just long enough to let the message be absorbed. Her address was constructed of a series of verbal headlines, each supported by brief, apt remarks. For variety, she used a story or humorous comment to break the almost hypnotic rhythm. Carol's respect for her grew as she watched the effortless control she exerted over her audience. And, even half-listening, Carol found herself mentally saying, Yes! when Marla said, "And as long as women see their only worth as approval in men's eyes, then their self-respect is built on sand . . ."

At the conclusion, as Marla raised her clenched fists in her trademark gesture, her audience rose in waves to clap, cheer, stamp their feet.

There was no overt threat to Marla's life: no assassin sprang up in the packed balconies to aim a rifle or lob a bomb; no fanatic tried to rush the stage; no killer was concealed in the corridors and rooms behind the hall to attack her after the performance concluded.

In the dressing room Marla was elated, and still talkative. Her enthusiasm even brought a chilly smile to Bev Diaz's lips. Pushing a glass of champagne into Carol's unwilling hand, Marla exclaimed, "You see, Carol! Nothing happened — and nothing will."

Carol put the champagne glass on the table. "One down," she said, "and ten more to go. If I were after you, I'd just watch you the first couple of times . . ."

CHAPTER FOUR

The quiet snick of a lock brought Carol instantly awake in the bedroom nearest the penthouse entrance. The illuminated clock showed ten past two. Wincing from the pain in her side, she slid off the bed and seized the flashlight and automatic she'd left ready. She eased off the safety catch as she padded to the half-open door, the loose cotton track suit whispering against her skin. She stepped into the spacious lounge area of the penthouse suite holding the flashlight well away from her body. If the dark figure by the door fired toward the sudden illumination, the bullet would, in the worst case, strike her left arm.

She pressed the switch. "Don't move!" The lance of light fell upon the startled features of Beverly Diaz, who immediately threw up an arm to shield her eyes. "Keep your hands where I can see them."

The woman remained still while Carol turned on the room light, and only then did Beverly Diaz lower her arm. She stood straight, her shoulders back. Her black eyes glared. "Taking your job rather too seriously, Inspector? Had you forgotten there are Huntling guards outside in the corridor?"

Carol opened the door and glanced out. The guard in his dark blue uniform grinned at her sheepishly. "I know you said to alert you if anyone came, but I knew Ms. Diaz was staying here and she said she'd let herself in and not to disturb you."

"Please follow my directions, even if it's Marla Strickland herself. Is that understood?"

The guard nodded slowly. "Sorry."

As she closed the door, it made the same soft click that had awakened her. She put her gun into the pocket of her track suit pants, its weight sagging against her thigh. She looked up to meet the other woman's blank stare. "I wasn't aware you were out tonight, Ms. Diaz. You said you were going to bed when I last saw you."

"I changed my mind."

Carol felt the weight of her dislike and smiled. "A sudden whim, was it?"

"If you like."

"Would you mind telling me where you've been."

"Yes, I would."

Carol waited. Most people felt the impulse to fill in the silence, but Bev Diaz just stood there, her stance challenging. Carol picked up the flashlight. "Then there's nothing more to discuss."

"Seems that way."

Carol knew her spurt of anger at the woman's insolent tone didn't show on her face. "Good night, then." She turned back at the bedroom door to find Bev Diaz still staring at her. "And Bev," she said with deliberate emphasis on the name, "for security reasons, don't do it again."

"Security?"

Carol smiled pleasantly. "Next time you might get shot."

The coffee shop was nearly empty, so Sid Safer and Carol had a favored booth by the window. "Give me a break," said Safer, tipping a third heaped spoon of sugar into his cup, "you know there's only a couple of us assigned to the Strickland tour full time, so following the Diaz woman every time she slips away just isn't on."

Carol took a long swallow of her black coffee. She had slept fitfully after waking last night and needed a caffeine jolt to start the morning. "But you would know if Bev Diaz had friends, contacts, anything like that here in Sydney?"

"Maybe."

"Come on, Sid. Give."

He shielded his eyes. "Don't turn the Ashton charm on me, Carol. I won't be able to resist."

"I thought," said Carol lightly, "there was a new era of cooperation between federal and state law enforcement..." They both knew that in the past there had been considerable friction between the two bodies.

"She could have been going to an AA meeting."

"An alcoholic? That wasn't in her file."

Sid grinned at Carol's surprise. "What's interesting is that she doesn't seem to have any reputation or history of out-of-control drinking. No one at Strickland Enterprises seems to have ever noticed any problem with alcohol."

"So why the AA meetings?"

"Search me." He shrugged. "Maybe she's kept it well-hidden, or she thinks she might have a tendency to hit the sauce in the future. Then again, maybe she just uses the meetings to pick up men."

Carol signaled for a second cup of coffee. "Another syrup?" she asked him, looking with disfavor at the thick dregs in his cup.

"If you're buying."

Carol waited until they were served, then said, "How long has Bev Diaz been attending AA meetings?"

"As far as we know, about a year."

"How did you find this out?"

Sid ran his fingers through his fair hair. "We have our sources." He grinned at her expression. "After the letter bomb we sent agents over to question Strickland office workers. It came up as background information. Apparently it became common knowledge that Diaz had started to go to Alcoholics Anonymous meetings."

"I can't imagine an AA meeting would keep her out until two o'clock in the morning."

He chuckled. "Hey, Carol. Maybe she found the man of her dreams."

"If so," said Carol, "her bliss didn't show."

Later that morning she ran into Marla's stepson in the penthouse kitchen. "Gary, I'd like a few words."

"Inspector." He slumped against a bench, smoothing his thin brown mustache as he waited for her to continue.

"Please call me Carol."

"Carol."

She hadn't known him long enough to decide if the hint of insolence in his tone was deliberately aimed at her, or was habitual. His face was soft and immature, his dull brown hair flopped over his forehead and he wore his usual expression of world-weary endurance. To prod him a little, she said, "You've done other tours with your mother?"

He straightened. "You mean Marla. My mother's dead."

"She died when you were quite young?"

Carol already knew the answer from briefing papers. Gary Hawkins had been six when his mother died and his father had waited six years before remarrying. It had also been Marla's second marriage — her first, a childless union, had ended in an acrimonious divorce.

"Why ask questions you already know the answer

to?" said Gary with surprising insight. He shoved his hands into the pockets of his grubby jeans. "So what do you really want to know?"

"What exactly are your duties? I know what they're supposed to be. I want to know what they *are.*"

He grinned, showing even, white teeth. "Yeah, sounds pretty grand to call me Transport Manager. The truth is, I'm Marla's gofer. I do anything she can't get anyone else to do . . . Or things she doesn't want anyone to know about." His mouth quirked resentfully. "Sort of keep it in the family."

Intrigued, Carol said mildly, "What sort of things would they be?"

Sly laughter put vitality into his face and he suddenly looked harder and more intelligent. "Nothing you'd be interested in, Carol." He put a deliberate emphasis on her name. "Though who knows, now that we're pals, I just might tell you . . . But not now. I've got to go."

You little bastard, Carol thought, undecided whether to be amused or irritated.

Room service provided lunch, although Marla complained that she'd much rather go down to the hotel's justly famous restaurant. She exclaimed impatiently when Carol insisted that the loaded dinner cart be brought in by a Huntling guard. "You don't think the waiter's going to have a gun, do you?"

Carol raised her eyebrows. "You obviously don't watch witness protection movies — it's a time-honored method to get access to the target."

Gary was the only one to join them for lunch, and he put his head down and ate single-mindedly, leaving the table as soon as he had finished.

Her good humor restored by the excellence of the food, Marla poured coffee for Carol and herself. She leaned back to regard Carol benignly. "Are you coming to the Art Gallery with me, or am I blessed with Anne Newsome?"

"It'll be my privilege."

Marla smiled at Carol's dry tone. "Art's not your thing?"

"On the contrary, art was one of my better subjects at school, and when I met Pat James I started taking an interest in exhibitions at the New South Wales Art Gallery."

"You know the curator of the Women Artists exhibition?" Marla was politely astonished.

Carol looked at her levelly. "Pat's married to one of my colleagues."

An incredulous smile. "Cops with culture!"

Carol's expression remained neutral, but inwardly she simmered. Just when she was on the verge of actually starting to like the woman, Strickland fired off a gratuitous insult. "Please wear your bullet-proof vest this evening," Carol said.

"Godammit! That thing is hot."

Carol thought how different the results would have been if *she* had been wearing protection when the kid had fired at her as she stood on the shabby suburban veranda. "Just wear it!" she said more savagely than she intended.

Marla surprised her by grinning. "Okay." She added, "But I'd like to know if it's worth the trouble — it doesn't stop everything, does it?"

Carol leaned over to pour herself another half cup of coffee. "No, but the layers of kevlar will deflect all but high velocity bullets, and it's a good protection against grenade or bomb fragments. It probably won't be much help in a knife attack, because it can be punctured."

"In that eventuality, perhaps I'll have to rely on *you*," said Marla mockingly.

Carol continued as if she hadn't spoken. "And if someone does shoot you, the blow will be like the kick from a horse. You'll have bruising, and maybe broken ribs."

"I'll wear it to please you, but no one's going to attack me."

"That," said Carol, "could be a famous last word."

"I trust you to protect me." Her tone was sardonic. "So I expect you to stop anyone — presuming there is such a person — getting close enough to hurt me."

Putting down her coffee cup, Carol said, "Did you know that Bev Diaz attends AA meetings?"

Marla's face darkened. "What business is that of yours?"

"Did you know?"

"Whatever Bev does — it's her concern. She's excellent at her job. That's enough for me." She pushed herself away from the table.

Carol tilted her head. "That's not an answer."

As she strode out of the room Marla snapped over her shoulder, "It's all you'll get, so drop it."

The Art Gallery sat floodlit in a sea of grass, its columned portico and sandstone walls glowing warmly in the fading light. Fruit bats flapped clumsily in the huge Morton Bay fig trees, the noise of their chattering clear in the cool evening air.

Gary Hawkins looked bored, but Marla leaned forward expectantly as the limousine drew up at the entrance. "Bev, have you got my notes?"

Bev Diaz tapped a black leather folder. "They're here, but you know you don't need them — you've got your prompt cards for the speech."

"I want you near me when I start, there might be a difficult question."

Carol was fascinated by this sign of insecurity in a woman who projected such an in-control persona. She said, "Do you need this preparation? You must have made hundreds, if not thousands, of speeches."

Marla shrugged. "I've learned you can't be too prepared. There's always someone with a question you haven't thought of, and if you're caught, it undermines everything you've said before."

Although Marla clearly intended to pause for the television cameras set up at the entrance, Carol hurried her up the steps to the portico, where Pat, red with embarrassed pride, waited with the director of the gallery and Joseph Marin, the ubiquitous Minister for Culture. Carol was surprised to see the New South Wales Minister for Police, Marjory Quince, standing beside him. The importance of the occasion had subdued Pat's usual springy enthusiasm, but she shot a quick smile to Carol before shaking Marla Strickland's hand.

The official party began a slow inspection of the exhibition, Joseph Marin constantly interrupting the director by making knowledgeable comments about women's art in Australia. Carol knew she had back-up — the demurely dressed Denise Cleever had unobtrusively joined the group — so she could spend a little time looking at the paintings.

She recognized some of the artists' names: Margaret Preston, Grace Crowley, Grace Crossington Smith, Thea Proctor — but there were many that were quite unfamiliar.

When the group stopped to admire a particularly striking Crossington Smith, Carol edged up to Pat. "Mark didn't make it?"

"I suggested it, but he said, No way." Pat's plain face was transformed by an affectionate smile. "Mark really is a virgin where art's concerned. Besides, he said he was, to quote him, *afeared* of Marla Strickland."

There was a chuckle behind them. "Afeared?" said Marla, "that's cute!"

Pat turned with a grin. "That's power — to make strong men weak."

Marla was suddenly serious. "No, it isn't. I want women strong — not men weak."

"I couldn't agree more!" Joseph Marin's hearty voice broke in. "Strong women. Strong men. Together we can build a strong society."

"Polly-speak," whispered Pat to Carol. "They just can't help it."

"And the family is the cornerstone of society," the minister announced.

"Then you'll be interested in my speech," said Marla with a cutting smile. "I mention the family several times."

The official party adjourned to a large room where invited guests were already indulging in food, drink and desultory conversation. They fell silent as Marla Strickland stepped onto a small podium to be introduced. As she began her address, Carol watched the guests' expressions of polite interest change to more genuine responses. Marla's subject was the dearth of women artists' names in the history of art, her theme the demands of a society so structured that it denied women the time to be artists, architects, composers. The only person who seemed impervious to the speaker was her stepson, Gary, who leaned casually against the door jamb with arms folded. Carol noticed Bev Diaz near the podium, and that Marla glanced at her now and then. It was, she decided, just a confidence booster. Marla didn't refer to notes, and spoke fluently without any hesitation or awkward pauses.

Although her voice exhibited her usual vibrant energy, her gestures were appropriately less theatrical for the smaller venue. With a mocking glance at Joseph Marin, she commented on the part the institution of the traditional family had played, with its rigid division of gender roles, so that power resided with males and time-consuming "women's work" was scornfully devalued. ". . . and as for those women who, despite all the odds, *did* achieve excellence in the exercise of their talents — their names are largely lost to us. Why is this? Is it because these women's artistic work just wasn't up to standard? No! It is because throughout history it has been *men*, with economic, political and religious power, who have conferred recognition on individuals. It has been *men* who have written the histories of artistic achievements, *men* who have decided who would be remembered, and who would not . . ."

"I enjoyed your speech," boomed the minister, gesturing expansively. "For too long women have been denied the recognition that is theirs by right . . ."

"Gives a new depth to the word pompous," said Denise Cleever, joining Carol near the podium. She indicated Marjory Quince, who was murmuring something to the gallery's director. "Is your minister checking up on you, Carol?"

"Shouldn't think so — but, then again, I didn't know she was interested in art . . ."

When first appointed to the position of Minister for Police, Senator Marjory Quince, a hard-working, no-nonsense politician, had had Carol's approval, but then she'd used her political position to demand special favors for a friend involved in a case, and Carol's opinion of the woman had changed.

As if Marjory Quince sensed she was the subject of discussion, she looked over at Carol and Denise, broke off her conversation, and approached them.

"Inspector Ashton. How delightful to see you here." Her voice was sharp-edged, matching her angular body. Her glance flickered over Denise, and she gave a small nod of recognition, then she turned toward Carol in an obvious move to exclude the ASIO agent. "Inspector, if I might have a word . . ."

"Of course, but I —"

"I'm well aware of your duties, Inspector. I'm not asking you to leave the room."

Carol wondered what was going on behind the hard planes of the almost expressionless face. Carol had never been intimidated by toughness or the exercise of power, but this woman had both, plus a dispassionate coldness that even she found unsettling.

"The Commissioner, I know, has impressed on you the fact that we believe Marla Strickland is in definite danger of attack. It isn't enough for you to protect her, Inspector, should an attempt on her life indeed be made. Any potential threat should be stopped before it begins. I'm certain I don't need to remind you how even a failed terrorist undertaking would generate very unfavorable publicity." She paused. "I'm told the Prime Minister himself has commented on the negative political fallout such an event could cause." Before Carol could respond, Marjory Quince added, "I'm sure Ms. Strickland is in good hands . . ." A brief, frigid smile, and she was gone.

Denise, who'd remained within earshot, said, "Did I hear the Prime Minister mentioned?"

"Just as an embellishment." Carol looked thoughtfully after Marjory Quince as she left the room. "There's some hidden agenda here. I wish I knew what it was."

* * * * *

People were straggling out of the Art Gallery as Carol came out to signal Marla's limousine, one of several waiting to the right of the entrance. The driver, a Federal agent, was leaning against the vehicle smoking a cigarette. He waved to Carol, stepped on his cigarette, and climbed inside.

She'd turned back to collect Marla when the explosion slammed her against one of the sandstone columns of the portico. Deafened for a moment, she was conscious of searing heat, and debris raining down around her. Someone gripped her arm. Through the ringing in her ears she could hear Joseph Marin. "God! Was that *my* car?"

Carol didn't answer. She took one look at the shattered vehicle, burning fiercely with orange flames, then tore herself free to run back to Marla Strickland, who stood open-mouthed just inside the entrance. "Get back inside. Now!"

"What's happened?"

"Right now!" Carol's side was afire with pain, but she almost bodily carried Marla back into the gallery. "Denise?"

"I'm here. I've radioed for help."

"Help?" said Carol. "The guy in the car's past it, and God knows who else . . ."

CHAPTER FIVE

Saturday morning. Carol stood at the penthouse window and looked at the broad expanse of Sydney Harbour dotted with weekend sailors in their yachts. Whenever she was able, she reserved Saturday morning for the delightful task of picking up her son, David. She would listen indulgently as he went through the important events of his week and then they would plan what they would do with their weekend. Those plans had always included Sybil. The pain of her desertion had begun to dull a little, but all that Carol needed was David to ask when Sybil was coming back, or for an image of the three of them in some past happy time to surface, and Carol would be stabbed with grief again.

She sighed as the phone rang for what seemed the hundredth time. "Carol Ashton."

"It's about time, Carol. I've been trying to reach you for days. Didn't you get any of my messages?"

"Madeline, I'm sorry, but —"

"I know. You've had your hands full with Strickland and then the explosion last night. *Very* newsworthy — even I've been called into the station. Anything new on the bomb? You can trust me not to name you."

Carol grimaced. This was typical Madeline Shipley, wanting the inside track on a hot story so she could run the information on *The Shipley Report.* Her success in the savage world of tabloid television was due in part to her relentless networking, but also because she always protected her sources, to the point where once she'd been arrested for contempt of court for refusing to name an informant involved in a financial scandal.

"Come on, Carol," Madeline cajoled, "I'll make it worth your while . . ."

With a tired smile, Carol said, "You know it's an offense to offer a bribe to a police officer."

"I don't have money in mind." Madeline's voice had fallen to an intimate purr. "Something much more interesting."

Carol slumped into the nearest sumptuous armchair and gazed out at the harbor. She wished she could be down there on the water, the yacht heeling under a stiff breeze, her only concern avoiding a dunking. "The offer's hard to resist," she said lightly, "but you know I can't give you any information."

"The offer's still good, with or without the information."

Carol could imagine Madeline in her elegantly furnished office, her burnished hair disciplined, her mouth curved in an easy smile. "Thanks, but no thanks."

Her refusal didn't offend. "You'll come round. In the meantime, I've got some information for *you*."

"To do with Marla Strickland?"

She straightened at Madeline's affirmative, "Ah-huh."

"What is it?" She grabbed a note pad and, cradling the receiver under her chin, unscrewed the cap of her gold fountain pen. "This is a murder case now, so give me anything you've got."

"First, Carol, I want a promise. If you can, you'll give me an exclusive when something breaks. Okay?"

"Okay, but no guarantees."

A chuckle came down the line. "If you weren't my favorite detective-inspector, I'd never do this for you, but I hear a murmur on the grapevine that someone or something called Wellspring is involved in the campaign against Strickland's tour."

Carol scribbled down the name. "Wellspring? One word?"

"I presume so. This is nothing concrete, just a whisper that I've picked up. And don't lean on me, Carol. There's nothing more to tell you."

"I'd like some names."

As she expected, Madeline snorted. "No names.

They wouldn't be any use to you anyway. But if you get a message to call me, you *will* answer it straight-away, won't you? I might get something more . . ."

She shook her head as she put down the receiver. Madeline was incorrigible. Then she frowned at the name she'd written down. Madeline was also very reliable — she would only pass along something she thought was significant.

"What did the doctor say?"

Carol looked up as Sid Safer was led in by a twitchy Pam Boyle, who, although taller than the federal officer, had hunched her shoulders until she was almost the same height. Carol said, "About me?"

He grinned. "Of course. You took some of the force of the blast. Strickland was inside the gallery, and besides, she's far too tough to have hysterics."

Carol thought of Marla's white-faced silence. "Not as tough as all that. She had to have something to sleep. As for me, all I've got is a few bruises and a superficial burn on one arm."

Safer looked at Pam, who was lingering by the door. "Could I have coffee? Milk and three sugars."

Today Pam Boyle had her frizzy brown hair tied back in a bulbous ponytail. She pulled at this as she stared at him. Just when it seemed obvious she was going to refuse to do anything so menial, she said, "Just this time," and disappeared through an inner door.

With a grunt, Sid hitched up the knees of his crumpled brown suit and settled himself down on a sofa near Carol's armchair. "Where's Strickland?"

"Marla and Bev Diaz are going through her speech for her next appearance. The curtains are drawn and I've told them to keep away from the windows."

"We're checking possible sniper positions in the surrounding office buildings, but the aspect of this apartment makes it almost impossible for anyone to get a clear shot."

Carol leaned back, rubbing her forehead. She'd had a pounding headache since the bomb had exploded, although the doctor had ruled out concussion. "Have you ever had anything to do with Marjory Quince?"

He looked surprised. "Your esteemed minister? Not really. Why?"

"After Marla's speech at the Art Gallery, Quince made a point of coming over to tell me that the Prime Minister, no less, was worried that even an abortive terrorist attempt would have unfortunate political repercussions. Then, a few minutes later, what happens . . ."

"So Quince gets lucky. Maybe she's psychic." Clearly he didn't consider the point very important. He gestured towards the inner rooms. "I presume Strickland's screaming for security to be beefed up?"

"On the contrary, she says she's quite satisfied, notwithstanding the attempt on her life —"

"If it *was* intended to kill her."

"Meaning?"

He leaned forward, elbows on his knees. "You'll get a full written report, but I can give you most of the info now. When not in use the limo was parked in a secure area and, as we do on a daily basis, we checked it out fully, inside and out, including a visual inspection of the underside, before you were picked up from the hotel and driven to the Art Gallery. There was no bomb."

"Could the driver have been carrying explosives?"

"You mean suicide or accident? Ken West was with the Federal Police for thirteen years. I knew him well and would have trusted him with my life. Ken couldn't be bought and he was very careful. Besides, the scientific evidence doesn't show the point of blast being the driver's seat. It was attached to the back left wheel arch of the vehicle." He went on with technical details of the plastic explosive and the detonation device used. ". . . which means that while the limo was parked with the others outside the gallery, someone took the opportunity to attach the bomb."

"One of the drivers?"

He smiled without humor. "Very good, Carol. There's one extra limousine and driver we can't account for. Unfortunately we've only got the vaguest of descriptions — just an average guy that no one noticed particularly. In the confusion after the blast he drove off." He paused while Pam Boyle came in with his coffee, slapping it down on the low glass table so that some slopped into the saucer. "We don't have sugar, only artificial stuff. It'll have to do."

"Thanks for going to the trouble."

He sounded sincere, and she wriggled her hunched shoulders. "That's all right."

Carol waited until she'd left the room. "You said it might not be an attempt on Marla's life."

"It was almost certainly a radio-detonated bomb, but Strickland wasn't anywhere near the vehicle when it blew. I don't think she was meant to die."

"I do wish you'd call me Marla!" She strode into

the room, followed by a grim Bev Diaz. "And what do you mean the bomb had nothing to do with me? Who else could have been the target?"

Her indignation made Sid laugh. "Calm down. I didn't say the bomb had nothing to do with you. I said it wasn't meant to kill you." He sobered. "The fact that one of my men died and two bystanders were seriously injured is no doubt incidental."

Bev Diaz fixed him with her black gaze. "What was the point of the bomb, then?"

"A statement, a warning, something to make you stop the tour."

"Perhaps," said Carol, "it's Act One, Scene Two."

Marla raised her eyebrows. "Scene Two?"

"Scene One," said Carol, "was the letter bomb."

WELLSPRING Noun 1
. the source of a spring, stream. 2. original or main source of anything 3. a source of abundant supply (as wellspring of information)

Carol sat alone in the living room of her house, the light pouring through the windows. Sinker lay curled, purring, on her lap. The wind whipped the foliage crowding the wooden deck, creating a sea of sound. The arch of sky above the eucalyptus gum trees was pale blue streaked with shredded cloud. She sighed and stretched carefully, her headache at last gone. She'd left Anne and Sid Safer in charge of Marla's safety for the afternoon and had hurried to the healing familiarity of her own home.

The coffee table was crowded with papers and a

bulky professional tape deck. Both ASIO and the Federal Police had come up with a blank on the name Wellspring, and inquiries overseas had also failed. There was no known political, religious or terrorist organization with the name, nor any using it as a codeword before detonating bombs.

Sinker complained as she leaned forward to punch the play button on the tape deck. Several calls had been made to talk-back radio stations on Friday afternoon and evening from people who had identified themselves as being with "Wellspring." She shut her eyes as the recorded messages began, willing herself to memorize every vocal characteristic. The tapes from the radio stations had already been enhanced by technicians, so each voice had a startling immediacy. In each case the mandatory ten-second broadcast delay had been activated once the program producer had realized what was happening, so that the full messages had not been broadcast.

The first one was a man, his voice deep and cultured. *"I am privileged to call you on behalf of Wellspring . . ."*

The talk-back announcer, over-hearty, cut in. *"And what are your thoughts on this hour's topic? Is feminism a necessary evil?"*

"Marla Strickland's message is like a virulent disease, infecting our society. Wellspring will purge the evil by destroying this loathsome woman. She has forfeited her right to live."

The second talk-back call had been made by a female, soft-voiced, but with the fire of conviction in her tone: *"I speak for Wellspring —"*

"I'm sorry, we don't allow political organizations to make statements on this program — this is for the general public . . ."

"Wellspring is speaking for the general public. We are forced to use cleansing fire to awaken everyone to the abomination that is Marla Strickland. She must be destroyed so that —" The producer had cut the caller off in mid-sentence.

The third, a male voice, was even more direct: *"Wellspring will smite Strickland tonight."*

As the tape rewound Carol glanced through the brief reports from a sound technician, a linguist and one of her own department's audio experts. All the callers had English as their native language. The first man was almost certainly British or had been educated in that country; the others were Australian, although the linguist detected a slight suggestion of an accent, possibly American, in the second speaker's voice. Voice prints had been made, but were clearly of no use without suspects for comparison.

"Didn't expect you home!" Aunt Sarah bustled in, laden with bulging department store bags. "Been shopping," she said unnecessarily, dumping everything on the sofa. "Sydney's a paradise compared to Leura . . ." She came around to look over Carol's shoulder. "Did you call London?"

"Sybil wasn't there. I left a message for her to call back."

"What are you going to say to her?"

Carol smiled ironically, "How about: Come Home All Is Forgiven?"

Aunt Sarah tapped her on the shoulder. "You

have to talk things out. You can't just ignore her and hope the problem will go away. You've done that too often, Carol."

"You sound like the police trauma therapist I had to go to after the shooting." She could visualize the therapist's homely, attentive face. "I only went because it's official police policy."

"Don't be defensive, dear. Everyone can do with a bit of counseling now and again."

Carol gave her an affectionate one-armed hug. "With you around, who needs a therapist?"

The phone rang. Sinker made outraged comments as she removed him from her lap. Sybil's voice was as clear as if she were in Sydney, and not half a world away. "Hi. I've just got in."

Carol shut her eyes. A surge of longing caught her breath. She could see Sybil's red hair and the way light caught her cheekbones. "I miss you."

"Me too."

"Then why didn't you call? Letters from you listing the tourist attractions of London aren't enough."

"Carol, I've got to make it here — by myself. I'll weaken if I speak to you too often."

"So *weaken*."

Sybil's laugh was rueful. "That's what's been wrong. I've been too weak for you, and worse, for me."

"That's not true," Carol contradicted her, even as she recognized the statement's validity.

"Of course it's true." When Carol was silent, she went on, "How's David? And Aunt Sarah?"

"David's on holiday in Bali with his father and Eleanor." She glanced at the postcard of a Bali sunset she'd put up on the kitchen noticeboard. "I got a postcard from him, and you can expect one too — he's got your address."

"When you see him, give him my love and tell him I'm writing."

"Sybil, I..." Carol couldn't find the right words.

"Is Aunt Sarah looking after you?" Sybil's voice was determinedly bright.

"She's spoiling me, as usual. And she sends her love."

"Give her mine." She paused. "I've been worried about you. The attempt on Marla Strickland's life's been big news here in London."

Carol said in a carefully conversational tone, "The way I feel tonight, I could resign tomorrow, and join you in London next week..."

Silence. Then, "That wouldn't work, Carol."

"Thanks for the comprehensive rejection."

"Oh, darling..." Sybil sounded at a loss. "What would you *do* in London after you'd been a tourist for a while? Most of the time I'm in lectures or doing field work."

Carol felt tired, defeated. "You really don't want me there, do you, even if I resign?"

"No. And you won't do it because it's not in your personality to run away from things."

"Is that a character reference?" she asked with a cynical laugh. Then, with a change of tone, "Sybil, what are we going to do?"

"I'm not sure. If we ever get together again, it has to be different for both of us. In the meantime, there are no strings, okay?"

"No strings?"

Sybil laughed softly. "You know exactly what I

mean, Carol. No strings. You're a free woman — and so am I."

She found Aunt Sarah in her bedroom unpacking the fruits of her shopping expedition. "How was Sybil?"

"She's fine. She sends her love." Carol was caught unaware by an odd exhilaration. "She says I'm a free woman . . ."

Aunt Sarah looked up. "That was wise of her." She went back to the shopping bags. "I've bought you a few things, dear. Your clothes are too sober. You need brightening up."

Carol tried to look grateful. Last time her aunt had decided to enhance Carol's wardrobe she'd been forced to endow the Salvation Army with a succession of impossibly garish garments. "Right now, I'd rather blend into the background."

Aunt Sarah's enthusiasm waned. "You're right, of course," she said. "The last thing you want to be is a target . . ."

CHAPTER SIX

Early on Sunday morning Carol opened the door of Marla Strickland's penthouse to an animated Pam Boyle, who brushed past her with an armful of Sunday newspapers. She had forgotten to hunch her shoulders and dip her head, and she even looked directly at Carol. "You can't *buy* this kind of publicity!" She dumped the papers on a table and ran her fingers over her hair, trying to flatten its springy wildness. "Where's Marla? She'll want to see this."

"Having breakfast in the sunroom."

Carol glanced at the headlines. They ranged from

the tabloid, MARLA MOCKS BOMB PERIL to the more restrained, and just as misleading, FEMINIST BOMB THREAT.

"No competition in the news this weekend, so we made the front pages," Pam exulted.

Carol was fascinated by the change in the woman. When she stood erect with her shoulders back, Pam was more than a head taller than Carol, and her unaccustomed stance revealed a more than adequate figure under the shapeless clothes she favored. Suddenly she seemed aware that she was out of character, pulling her shoulders forward as she scooped up the newspapers. "I'll take them in."

The phone gave a discreet burr. Carol picked it up. "Who? Okay . . ."

A click, and Madeline Shipley's assured voice said, "Carol? You know your charge is on my program tomorrow night. I thought we might have a personal meeting to discuss security at the studio."

She had to laugh. "Do you ever give up, Madeline?"

"You've asked me that before, so you know I don't. Besides, after that bomb on Friday night, things seem a little more serious than just threats, don't they?"

"Yes they do, and that's why I want Marla to pre-record your program. She won't agree — she wants to go to air live — but I thought you might try to persuade her."

"I must admit I like the immediacy of a live interview, but I'll do it earlier in the day if you can change her mind." The warmth intensified in her voice. "I *would* like to see you."

Carol thought of the conversation with Sybil. "I've got some free time tomorrow. Maybe we could meet."

"Somehow I knew you'd say that . . ."

Carol was looking thoughtfully out the window at the tiny people on the street below when the phone rang again. "Yes . . . Send him up."

Five minutes later there was a firm knock on the door. "Huntling Security." He handed Carol his card. "I'm Keil Huntling. My sister and I run the company." His smile was broad and confident, his voice deeply resonant. "We've been in the field for over ten years and you'll be aware that we've been fully checked out by both ASIO and the Feds."

Wondering why he was so anxious to establish the company's credentials when he must know that she would already have the information, Carol nodded pleasantly and waited to see what further reassurance he would give.

He looked around the penthouse entertainment area. It was furnished in simple luxury, allowing the stunning views from the floor-length windows to complete the impression of understated affluence. "Very nice." His pale gray suit was impeccable, his white shirt crisp, his deep red tie the only touch of color. He matched his photograph in the file on Huntling Security, but Carol automatically ran through her usual checklist: average height, broad-shouldered, muscular build, very short brown hair, heavy jaw, ruddy complexion, pale blue eyes, stubby fingers, no rings. He cleared his throat. "Is Ms. Strickland available?"

"I'm afraid not." She didn't mention that Marla was luxuriating in a sunken marble bath before having a manicure and facial from a beautician. As she'd left the penthouse, Anne Newsome had made a wry comment about the politically correct feminists who'd criticize such self-indulgence.

He gestured to the flat maroon briefcase he held under one arm. "It's just that we need to go over some security details." He gave Carol a conspiratorial smile, which she didn't return. "Of course security matters are really the province of people like yourself, Inspector, but, as I'm sure you know, Ms. Strickland is hands-on — and we like to keep her happy." He looked around. "Do you mind if we sit down?"

Carol gestured to the chairs set around a low table near the window. He unbuttoned his suit coat before he sat down, then his thick fingers wrenched at the zipper of the briefcase. "I'm sure there'll be cancellations and changes after what happened at the Art Gallery . . ."

"There's no change to the itinerary."

Keil Huntling raised his eyebrows. "No? But all the publicity . . . every nut will be coming out of the woodwork."

Nodding agreement, Carol thought of Marla's obstinacy at the suggestion that, at the very least, some of her media appearances be curtailed. She'd consented to taking the weekend off, but the rest of her engagements were to remain the same.

Huntling shuffled the papers he'd taken out. "We're scanning all postal items and, naturally, any parcels or letters delivered to the hotel. There's been a distinct increase in volume since the attempt on her life . . ."

Irritated by his self-importance, Carol said, "But no letter bombs."

"Threats. There've been threats, Inspector."

Carol had seen each day's breakdown of items received. "And a lot of supportive messages, too."

"Under the circumstances, I suggest we tighten security to red alert status." He sat back, his manner indicating he expected her full support for the suggestion.

A cold voice broke in. "Red alert, Mr. Huntling?" Bev Diaz had approached them, silent on the thick blue carpet. "Am I correct in assuming that would mean more money for your company?" Her expression indicated her contempt for such a notion.

He stood, spreading his hands. "There'd be more Huntling staff involved, of course, but what does cost matter if you have total security?"

"It matters a lot. And there's no such thing as total security." Bev Diaz smiled unpleasantly. "And if you don't know that, you're in the wrong business."

Her enmity left him standing there awkwardly. Carol rescued him. "Mr. Huntling has security details he wants Marla to see."

Bev Diaz put out her hand. "I'll see she gets them."

Unwillingly, he passed the papers to her. "I would like to see Ms. Strickland personally."

"You're a bit player in this," said Bev, her dark eyes blankly antagonistic. "The only reason Marla wanted your company is that it is headed by a woman. I would recommend you send your *sister* if there's any necessity for personal contact."

"Pam Boyle liaised directly with Cynthia —"

"I'm Ms. Strickland's personal assistant. I strongly suggest that your sister contact *me* if there's any problem."

"There's no problem," he hastened to reassure her. "Everything's under control."

"Then I fail to see why this visit was necessary."

When the door closed behind him, she turned to Carol. "Think I was too hard on him?" Her tone was a challenge.

Carol grinned. "I'm sure *he* thinks so."

Bev's face relaxed a little. "I'd rather rely on professionals like you."

"Is that a compliment?"

She didn't seem to mind the edge of irony in Carol's voice. "You do your job." Unexpectedly, she added, "I like Anne Newsome."

Surprised at her comment, Carol said, "Why do you like Anne?"

Bev shrugged. "She's down to earth. Doesn't talk too much." She paused. "I trust her." When Carol didn't comment, she added with a faint, rueful smile, "And, frankly, I don't trust many people."

Nor do I. Carol felt the possibility of friendship flicker between them. It was the first time Bev had revealed anything of herself. "Like a coffee? I'm getting myself one."

Bev hesitated, then said, "Sure. Why not?"

Carol had scheduled a mid-afternoon meeting in the penthouse to discuss the latest information about the Art Gallery bombing. Pam Boyle slid the laden tray onto the low table. "I put on a plate of cookies," she said with the air of one giving a considerable concession. She stood back as everyone helped themselves to coffee, then didn't leave the room, but went to sit in a lounge chair near the bar. When Carol glanced at her she'd picked up a magazine and was apparently reading it closely.

Denise touched Carol's knee. "Keeping tabs on us," she said softly, with a nod towards Pam Boyle.

"As I was saying . . ." Sid Safer was holding court. "Our valuable Minister for Culture tells me he's convinced *he* was the intended target for the limo explosion. He wants to know every detail of what we're doing to find the mad bomber who wants to destroy him."

"Who would bother killing Joseph Marin?" Denise Cleever was scornful. "Except for a complete lack of common sense and any ability to manage his ministry, he's harmless."

Sid sat back, loosening his tie and undoing the top button of his shirt. "I agree he knows bugger-all about culture, but he's bright enough to play the numbers and become a federal minister."

"He played the prayer group," said Denise with derision. "God was on his side."

Carol, who'd been gazing at the soaring gray arch of the Sydney Harbour Bridge, came back to the conversation. "What prayer group?"

This daily meeting would, she knew, become routine as Marla's tour continued, its purpose to review security arrangements and plan for any specific hazards at future appearances. Denise and Sid seemed to have overcome the traditional wariness between law enforcement and the highly-secret ASIO, and had been trading flippant remarks since the meeting began.

Denise put her hands together in mock prayer. "You can be confident that the Almighty has an eye on Australia, since there's an early morning prayer meeting almost every day they're in session in Canberra. Only a couple of cabinet members belong, but there's quite a few backbenchers flinging themselves on their knees for their country. That's where Joseph Marin's influence comes from — the godly."

Carol leaned forward. "Fundamentalist Christian?"

"No. Any denomination. All you need is to say you believe in some sort of Supreme Being." Denise grinned. "I had the same thought, Carol, since it's the far right who hate Marla so much, but this lot are pretty ineffectual. Months ago, when Marin started squeaking that he was a terrorist target we double-checked everything and everybody. The prayer group is just that, and nothing more."

Sid swallowed the dregs in his cup and grabbed for the coffee pot. "Isn't there something similar in State Parliament? I remember vaguely that some columnist sent them up . . ."

Anne, who'd been sitting silently with an open notebook, broke in. "There is. It's the same as Federal Parliament — just a number of politicians from both sides who get together for prayer meetings."

Carol said, "Do you happen to know if Marjory Quince belongs?"

"Shouldn't think so," said Denise. "She doesn't strike me as the sort to see any political advantage in belonging — and that's the only thing that could motivate her to associate with such a wishy-washy group."

"To more weighty matters," said Sid, opening his battered brown briefcase. "We might just have a written contact from Wellspring." He handed around copies. "Mailed yesterday at Redfern, and delivered with commendable efficiency this morning."

Carol scanned the single page quickly.

We are Wellspring. We are the pure, untainted Word. We are perfect virtue and purity. We are self-denial and chastity. We are honor and decency. We are the conscience of society.

The flesh is weak. Greed, concupiscence and hedonism contaminate the world. The swinish wallow in carnality.

The woman Marla Strickland leads the innocent to destruction and approves the lechery of the corrupt. Mired in her degeneracy she seeks to destroy all order and natural morality.

Wellspring must destroy this woman and those like her so that we may all return to a state of cleanliness.

"I detect heavy use of a thesaurus," said Denise. "And an unhealthy dose of self-righteousness."

Sid flapped his sheet. "No fingerprints. Common heavyweight paper. Typed on a computer then run through an ink-jet printer. No saliva on the envelope — used a self-sealer and posted it with a self-adhesive stamp."

"Can we keep it quiet?"

Marla, towing a sullen-faced Gary Hawkins behind her, entered in time to hear Denise's question. "Keep what quiet? If it's about me, I should know about it."

Sid handed her a copy. "It appears to be the same group who called the radio stations."

Hawkins looked over her shoulder as she scanned the page. "Standard stuff," he said contemptuously.

"Bombing a car is a bit more than standard," said Sid.

Hawkins wasn't impressed. "Every goofball will be claiming responsibility. I can't see how you can be sure this Wellspring group had anything to do with it."

"They're our best bet at the moment." Sid turned to Marla. "If they did detonate that car bomb, they're more than dangerous."

She pursed her lips over the page. "I'd like to release this to the media."

"It's not very flattering," said Anne.

"It *is* publicity. And that's how you fight cowards like this — you put them in the full glare of public opinion. I'm on *The Shipley Report* tomorrow night. I'll release the full text then."

Sid leaned back to regard her admiringly. "You sure have balls!"

She looked at him with distaste. "If your security skills are in line with your knowledge of anatomy, we're in big trouble."

CHAPTER SEVEN

The next morning Madeline opened the front door before Carol had time to ring the bell. Her face was bare of makeup and she wore a loose T-shirt with the logo of her television station on it and faded blue jeans. This was so unlike Madeline's usual elegant clothing that Carol looked at her appraisingly. Her tantalizing smile, rich copper hair and deep gray eyes were on the screen five days a week in *The Shipley Report* and her image was ubiquitous on billboards and in advertisements. Familiarity had made Carol forget what a beautiful woman Madeline was.

"Carol, I've been watching for you." She was matter-of-fact, without the playful coquetry that characterized most of their conversations. "I —" She made an impatient gesture. "Come in."

Following her down the hall, Carol was scalded by memory of the last time she'd been in this house. Madeline had been in control then, had seduced her — and she'd been a willing accomplice. She'd never been sure what might have happened next, because Sybil had returned to her, and Madeline had gracefully retreated to their former relationship of edgy friendship.

As they entered a sitting room with a glass wall overlooking the gardens, Carol said conversationally, "Have you heard from Paul?"

"He's gone for good, Carol. Our marriage was a sham — you know that. I haven't spoken to him for over a year." She gestured Carol towards a lounge chair. "Sit down, you intimidate me when you stand over me."

Carol laughed as she obeyed. "Nothing could intimidate you."

Madeline didn't smile. "Do you want coffee? A drink? Anything?" Her offer was perfunctory, and she seemed relieved when Carol shook her head. She didn't sit, but stood looking at Carol reflectively. "Tell me about Sybil."

"She's in London for a year." An easy, conversational tone.

"She's left you for the second time. Is it permanent this time?"

"I can't say."

"Do you want her back?" Seeing the protest on

Carol's face, she added quickly, "Carol, please. I wouldn't be asking you if it wasn't important."

Carol felt an unwanted tingle of excitement. She didn't want the friendly sparring to change, but her body remembered with disconcerting intensity the touch of Madeline's fingers. "I really can't answer that. All I can say is I miss her very much."

"This is more important to me than I ever meant it to be." Madeline smiled ruefully as she spread her hands, "You've got through to me in a way I never expected. It isn't just sex . . ." She raised an eyebrow. "Though that one time was pretty sensational."

"I don't know what to say," said Carol lightly.

"Sure you do. You just don't want to say it." Madeline stepped forward to lean over her, hands resting on the armrests so that Carol was imprisoned.

Carol looked up at curved lips so enticingly close. "Madeline, I don't . . ."

She laughed softly. "You don't? I want it enough for both of us."

Madeline's mouth was fire, her kiss igniting a rush of heat. Carol resisted the urge to pull her down into a full embrace, but could not prevent her body's dizzying response. Too soon, Madeline drew back.

Carol had expected Madeline's usual mocking smile, but she was somber, serious.

They stared at each other, and Carol was aware that this was a turning point, where possibilities shimmered. She said, "What is it you want?"

Looking down into her face, Madeline said quietly, "Oh, nothing much. I want you to be in love with me, Carol, that's all."

* * * * *

The security at Channel Thirteen was tight, but Carol still felt relieved when Marla was safely in the studio. Bev Diaz, who had accompanied them, obviously felt the same way. She allowed her ramrod stance to relax slightly as she said to Carol, "Thank God we're here safely."

Carol nodded. Even though she knew their transport vehicle — an anonymous dark sedan — had been double-checked for explosive devices, she could still see the fiercely burning wreck of the limousine outside the Art Gallery.

Bev looked over at Madeline Shipley, who was on the set talking to the floor manager. "You know her?"

"Yes, she's a friend." *More than a friend?* "Madeline's very supportive of women in public life and her show's extremely successful, so it's an opportunity for women to be heard." Carol smiled wryly to herself. *I'm starting to sound like a card-carrying feminist.*

Bev's cupid-bow mouth tightened. "Would she be so successful if she were plain, or ugly?"

"Apart from her looks she's intelligent and talented."

"That's enough for a woman in television, is it?" Bev's black eyes challenged.

Carol conceded, "It helps to be good-looking." Irritated that she felt she needed to justify this statement, she said curtly, "It's a fact of life that the general public is drawn to attractive people. And wouldn't you admit that as individuals we are, too?"

Bev's reply was forestalled by Madeline, who came

off the set to greet them. She smiled at Carol, shook Bev Diaz's hand and then turned to Marla. "It's wonderful to meet you in person. I know we've already discussed the questions on the phone, but is there anything else you'd like to cover?"

Carol stood back, feeling a tug of excitement in the contrast between the Madeline Shipley she had seen that morning and this familiar polished performer whose charm seemed as natural as breathing. *For me you're different. For me.*

If Madeline was aware of her scrutiny, she showed no sign of it. Her attention was all for Marla. "This segment tonight will be a great teaser for my in-depth program on you and your impact on Australian feminism, and I'm excited you've chosen *The Shipley Report* as your first official television appearance. We have the text of the Wellspring letter set up for on-screen, but are you aware that other media outlets got copies this afternoon? It means we haven't got an exclusive . . ."

"But you've got *me*," said Marla.

There was no live audience for the show. Carol was offered a battered metal chair, but declined. The studio floor was a tangle of cables and leads, the cameras brooded like huge metal birds, the floodlights were blindingly bright. The floor crew, most of them alarmingly young, were calm in the seeming chaos. Behind glass in the control booth several people were hunched over panels covered in dials and switches. Sid Safer's comforting presence loomed behind them.

She looked at the island of light that was the set. On the screen its clean lines looked expensively solid: in reality it was surprisingly flimsy. Watching Madeline's attentive expression as she waited for the floor manager to count down the final seconds of the commercial, Carol grimaced. Her response to Madeline's declaration that morning had been so ungracious, resentful. She had replayed her words a hundred times: "Don't spring this on me, Madeline. Give me time, okay?" They had parted, Carol giving her a quick embrace, then escaping gratefully to the refuge of her car. Now, hours later, she was still confused by her reactions. Attraction had previously been a game between them, and it wasn't fair that Madeline had changed the rules.

When the interview began Carol glanced up at the monitor. It was clear the camera loved both women — on the screen they glowed with larger-than-life vitality. The segment ran smoothly, with question and answer interspersed with footage of the burning limousine and scenes from the Town Hall meeting. The build-up to the revelation of the Wellspring letter was expertly done, and was followed immediately by Marla Strickland staring directly into the camera.

"... and I have this message for those psychotics who plant bombs and kill innocent people, for those cowards who send anonymous, poisonous messages ..." The camera went to extreme close-up as Marla spoke slowly and with total conviction. "When women stand together they cannot be harassed, they cannot be put down, they cannot be silenced. And *I* will not be harassed, *I* will not be put down, *I* will not be silenced. Nothing, and no one, can stop me speaking the truth about the inequalities that women suffer."

* * * * *

Marla was effervescent on the way back to the hotel. Carol screened out her comments, letting Bev Diaz be the audience. Although there were two unmarked escort cars, one in front and one behind, Carol was still tense, her fingers constantly brushing the comforting metal of the gun concealed under her jacket.

This time they were going to the front entrance of the hotel, rather than the back — it was important not to fall into a pattern that would make it easier for someone stalking a potential victim. Anne Newsome, accompanied by one of the Huntling guards, met them in the lobby. "You can leave, if you like, Carol. The penthouse is secure and I'll take Ms. Strickland straight up."

Carol nodded her thanks to Anne, said good night to Marla, then caught Bev Diaz's arm before she could join them. "Would you have a drink with me? There's something I'd like to discuss."

They found a booth in the hotel's sleekly modern bar and an attentive young waiter hurried over. Carol was curious to see if Bev Diaz would order alcohol.

"Coke, please."

He looked expectantly at Carol.

"Johnny Walker on the rocks." She turned back to Bev, who was sitting tautly, her back not touching the dark green leather of the booth. "The death of the driver at the Art Gallery means I'm asking questions I wouldn't have worried about before. And I expect answers."

Bev looked at her, expressionless. At last she said, "Do you enjoy your job?"

Carol was puzzled by the intent behind the

question. "Is that some sort of veiled threat, or is it an honest inquiry?"

"Honest." Her lips twitched. "I'm always honest, if I can be. I merely wanted to know if you like being a police officer."

It's my life, the structure of my day, the way I control my world. "Yes, I do . . . most of the time."

"And this isn't one of them?"

"I wouldn't choose to be a bodyguard."

Bev narrowed her eyes. "You didn't volunteer, of course, so that means someone wanted you for the job. It certainly wasn't Marla — you know her opinion — so who made the decision?"

Who indeed ? "It's not relevant."

"It is if you're not the best for the job. Maybe someone in authority wants Marla dead, so a second-rate bodyguard gets appointed."

"I won't take that personally," Carol assured her.

The woman opposite her relaxed a little. "I'm probably becoming paranoid and looking for plots everywhere. Marla's taking it in her stride, but I . . ." A shrug finished the sentence.

The waiter glided up to deposit their drinks with reverent precision. Carol waited until he'd gone. "Why do you go to AA meetings?" The blunt question skidded off Bev's armored expression. She picked up her Coke and took a long swallow. Carol said, "Are you an alcoholic?"

"Is that important?" Bev sounded weary.

"I'd like to know if you're attending AA meetings in Sydney."

Bev put her glass down deliberately. "I'm attending AA meetings. Okay?"

"Your profile doesn't mention alcoholism. "

Bev made preparations to go. "What's your problem?"

"There are AA meetings in every city and town. Only first names are used and everyone identifies himself or herself as an alcoholic and is made welcome. No one has to justify being there, and talking to strangers is part of the process. It's a perfect place to pass information."

Bev settled back, her eyes glittering. "Just what are you saying?"

"If I were running Wellspring," said Carol reflectively, "I'd position someone close to the target for inside information."

Bev looked at her for a long moment. "And you think I'm that someone?" She didn't wait for Carol's response, leaning forward to say with quiet intensity, "You can think what you like — it doesn't concern me. I believe in everything that Marla Strickland stands for. She speaks for *me,* and for countless women like me." Without another word she gathered her things and strode out of the bar.

Carol watched her departure thoughtfully. *Wouldn't I say exactly that, if I were a plant?*

Early on Tuesday morning Carol collected Olga, her neighbor's German shepherd, and tried a gentle jog on what had previously been her running route through the bushland near her house. When she had come out of the hospital she'd been so weak and out of condition that even a leisurely stroll had exhausted her, but she had steadily built up to longer and more demanding walks until she was ready to ease into her customary running routine.

She returned home with the exhilarating realization that the strength and flexibility of her body was returning, even though the dull pain still nagged at her side.

After her shower she stood naked in front of the mirror. She was under her best weight and her face looked gaunt; the bruises from the explosion were dark blurs on her hip and arm; below her right ribs the scars from surgery were fading. She smiled at her reflection. The buoyant health she had taken for granted and the strength and grace of her body were returning.

Grimly, she traced the looping scars with her fingertips. She had nearly bled to death before the ambulance, siren screaming, had made it to the emergency room. She still dreamed of the blur of bright lights and pain and terrifying weakness that had made drawing each breath a grievous struggle. To have that happen again . . .

"Breakfast!" shouted Aunt Sarah, always at her energetic best in the morning. Carol put on a track suit and came out to find a large glass of orange juice waiting for her. "Drink. It's freshly squeezed." Aunt Sarah hovered in her deep purple house coat with lime green trim until Carol took her first gulp and made the appropriate appreciative noises.

"I had hoped David would be back before I go home to the mountains." She grinned at Carol. "There are some movies we haven't seen yet."

"Marla Strickland's talking of extending her tour. I may be begging you to stay longer if that happens."

"You need someone to live with you, anyway," said Aunt Sarah, scooping up Jeffrey and putting him under one arm.

"I'm perfectly all right by myself."

Her aunt's smile was mocking. "Heavens, I was thinking more of the *cats* — they need more company than you provide..." She slapped the morning papers down in front of her. "You can read these while I get you breakfast."

"I only want toast and coffee."

"Coffee! You'd be lucky!"

Both morning papers had given Marla extensive front page coverage, including the full text of the Wellspring letter and a rehash of the stories about the letter bomb in the States and the explosion at the Art Gallery. On the inside pages Marla was the subject of editorials: *US feminist a catalyst for conflict,* declared the broadsheet. The tabloid asked: *Do we need to import trouble-makers? We have enough feminazis of our own.*

Aunt Sarah successfully bullied Carol into fruit and cereal, but failed to stop her from drinking two mugs of black coffee. As Carol poured a third mug to take with her while she changed, her aunt exclaimed, "Your cholesterol, Carol! Not to mention irregular heart rhythms! You mustn't take your health for granted."

"I admit I used to. I don't anymore."

Aunt Sarah looked contrite. "Of course you don't." She patted Carol's hand. "I can't imagine how I forgot that only a few months ago you were in hospital." She rallied to add, "But that doesn't mean that you can completely ignore the studies that show that drinking coffee is tantamount to swallowing poison . . ."

Carol relieved Anne Newsome at eight-thirty. "Uneventful, I hope?"

Anne passed her the activity log. "Marla stayed in all evening." She grinned wickedly. "And Pam Boyle swooped around the apartment with knees bent, trying to look shorter. Gary Hawkins went out to 'look around,' as he put it, about ten last night. He must have had a good time, he wasn't back until after two."

"Say where he went?"

"I asked, but he told me to mind my own business. The same thing with the formidable Bev Diaz. She left the hotel about the same time, but was back here by midnight. *She* told me to get lost even more emphatically than he did."

Preparing to leave, Anne said, "You don't think there's any chance that someone here is feeding Wellspring information?"

Carol yawned. She'd lain awake for hours, and when she had fallen into an uneasy sleep her dreams had been full of disconnected images of Sybil and Madeline. "Having a person on the inside would be ideal."

Anne paused at the door. "Maybe La Strickland's engineering the whole thing for publicity."

"I heard that!"

"I'm going," said Anne, as Marla advanced in a swirl of cream satin dressing gown.

Marla halted, hands on hips. She eyed Carol's severely cut blue suit and gold jewelry. "Well . . . Getting dressed up, Inspector?"

"This afternoon you're speaking to More Women in Government in the Great Hall of Sydney University. I need to blend in with the crowd."

"Come and have coffee with me." She grinned back over her satin shoulder. "We can talk about the lengths I'll go to, to get publicity."

The sunroom was furnished in warm ocher tones and blond wood furniture. Pam Boyle, sitting at a desk in one corner bent over paperwork, glanced up as Carol entered, then pointedly went back to her reading.

In her imagination Carol could hear her aunt tut-tutting as Carol accepted her fourth coffee of the day. She took a long sip, then said, "It was a flippant remark. Anne didn't mean to imply —"

"I wouldn't kill for publicity, Carol. Other nefarious things, perhaps — but bombs are out." She looked at Carol over the rim of her cup. "These threats from Wellspring . . . If I die, I die."

"A martyr to the cause?" Carol's tone was light.

"That's right." She seemed completely sincere as she went on, "Every movement needs martyrs. The assassination of Martin Luther King is a case in point. His death, along with others, galvanized the civil rights movement."

"Are you serious?"

"Perfectly."

"Then," said Carol, "you certainly don't need a bodyguard. Quite the opposite."

Marla grinned at her wry tone. "I've given up on trying to have you removed. You're far too entertaining to lose." A frown replaced her smile as she added, "But I can't say the same for Sid Safer. I'd be happy to get rid of him."

Pam unwound herself and came over to perch awkwardly on the couch's arm. "Safer's okay, but I don't like Denise Cleever." She began to play with her hair, vainly trying to loop its thick, tightly-curled strands behind her ears.

Carol was curious. "Why don't you like her?"

"Her manner. She's rude."

"I've never noticed that."

Pam ignored her comment, speaking directly to Marla. "And Denise Cleever's a *lesbian*." The word was infused with loathing.

Carol raised her eyebrows. "So am I." She heard the echo of her words, and wondered how many times she'd avoided this admission in the past.

"Yes," said Pam with venom. "You are."

CHAPTER EIGHT

Sydney University, the oldest in Australia, was familiar to Carol from her student days. The Quad, formed by a square of impressive Gothic Revival architecture, was still carpeted with the same jewel-green grass. Today, the Great Hall, with the portraits of past chancellors gazing down importantly from its dark paneled walls, was filled with a talkative audience taking the opportunity to network.

The chairperson of MOWIG — More Women in Government — was an exquisitely dressed fluttery woman who seemed overwhelmed by the fame of her guest. She stood beside the dais with Marla and Carol, peering anxiously into their faces in turn. "I *do* hope everything will be all right! I mean, the sound system had a *serious* problem, but I believe that the technician has fixed it just in time . . ."

"I'll shout," said Marla.

Not sure if she was joking, the woman said hastily, "Oh, I'm sure that won't be necessary. The Great Hall has excellent acoustics, but it *is* quite large, actually . . ." She paused as a uniformed university guard hurried up. He bent to speak urgently in her ear. "Oh, my goodness! But —"

Her look of shock impelled Carol to take over. "What is it?" When he looked doubtful, she said impatiently, "I'm Inspector Ashton. Any security problems are supposed to come directly to me."

"There's a bomb threat just phoned through to the University. They said the Great Hall would be blown up at two-thirty."

Carol checked her watch. "A little less than twenty minutes." She looked back to the guard, who was visibly sweating. "Anything else?"

"They said to tell the speaker it was Wellspring." He looked around nervously. "They did the car bomb, didn't they?"

"Car bomb!"

Carol gripped the chairwoman's arm. The last thing Carol wanted the audience to hear was exclamations about bombs. "Don't say why, just insist that your committee members and anyone else in the official party leave by the back entrance." When she hesitated, Carol said firmly, "Right now."

Denise Cleever appeared beside them. "I've just

heard about the call. We had this place checked out this morning and it's been guarded ever since. There's nothing here — it has to be a hoax."

"But you've called the bomb squad?"

"Sure. You'll hear the sirens in a minute. And surrounding areas are being cleared."

Carol turned to the guard. "Go down to the entrance and get people out, fast. But don't panic them, and don't mention a bomb." To Denise she said, "Stay with Marla and take her out the back way, but be careful. This scare could be to get her outside so she's a clear target."

Carol stepped onto the dais and turned on the microphone at the speaker's desk. The anonymous technician had been efficient — her clear voice rang through the hall. "May I have your attention please. There's been a gas leak. I repeat, a gas leak. Just as a safety precaution, we must ask you all to leave the hall immediately." A murmur of consternation swelled. "And once outside, move well clear of the building." She looked at her watch. "This is a regulation evacuation, but we do have an optimum time for such drills. Please leave the hall as quickly as possible."

The whine of sirens grew louder as the audience filed out, many muttering about the inconvenience. Carol shepherded the stragglers, visually checking each row of seats for packages on or under them as she walked down the central aisle. It had been an invitation-only MOWIG audience and Marla had insisted that metal detectors were unnecessary. Someone in the audience could have brought in a bomb and armed it before leaving when the call to evacuate the hall was given. At the door she won a brief battle of wills with an indignant woman who'd left something behind and wanted to retrieve it, and then, with a wash of relief, she was outside. She'd seen bomb injuries, and retained nightmarish images of the damage explosives could do to soft human flesh.

Marla, along with Bev and Pam, had been taken to the administrative offices, and while the bomb squad searched the Great Hall she sipped mineral water and waited, refusing to return to the hotel. "As soon as the search is over I'm going back to give my speech. I don't care if only five people stay to see me, *nothing* is going to stop me from speaking."

MOWIG committee members seemed more robust than the chairwoman, who had twittered nervously at the suggestion that they return to the hall. "Excellent," said one, who had a brisk, no-nonsense manner that reminded Carol of a former head-mistress, "that's the way to show them women can't be intimidated by threats."

Denise, followed by an officer in a heavy flack suit, came into the office carrying a cardboard shoe box. "Carol, thought you'd like to know what was found. No bomb, but this . . ."

Inside the box was a brief, typed note:

THIS COULD HAVE BEEN A BOMB. KNOW YOUR DAYS ARE NUMBERED.

Neatly printed at the bottom of the page was one word: WELLSPRING.

"Melodramatic, aren't they?" said Denise.

* * * * *

Carol had arranged for the Wednesday meeting to be mid-morning, to give time for laboratory analysis of the shoe box and a photograph, still damp from processing, that had been delivered to the front desk of the hotel early on Tuesday evening. She opened the door of Marla's penthouse to Anne, Denise, and Sid Safer at ten-thirty.

Marla had already helped herself to a vodka and tonic. Now she was sitting with her second drink, staring morosely out of the window and apparently ignoring the discussion around her.

"Could Family First be a front for Wellspring?"

Denise considered Anne Newsome's question. "ASIO's files haven't got anything to link them. How about the Feds, Sid?"

A shake of his head. "Family First doesn't seem to have anything to hide, and individual members like to be publicly identified with the organization because it makes them obviously holier than the rest of us. As for Wellspring, we really don't know anything about them at all."

"Obviously they're opposed to everything Marla stands for, and then some," said Denise. "And murder isn't too much of an inconvenience," she added.

Carol thought of the limo driver. He'd served in the Federal Police for most of his adult life, had a wife and three children and could not have expected to die in blood and fire. "Anything further on the car bomb?"

"Plastic explosive. Radio detonated. Didn't need an

Einstein to make it, or set it off." The corners of Sid's mouth turned down. "In other words, we've got nothing."

Carol gestured to the photo that lay before her on the table. "And this?"

Sid pulled reflectively at his ear. "Anyone with access to a darkroom and an enlarger could have produced it. No particular expertise required." He sighed irritably. "And the taxi driver who delivered the envelope to the hotel was answering a telephone booking to a company called Silverwater Graphics. There was a woman waiting outside and she handed him the envelope and paid for the delivery with money she said was from petty cash. He didn't think anything of it, and his description's pretty vague — brown hair, middle-aged and neatly dressed. Needless to say, no one at the company knows anything about it."

"But you're checking out Silverwater Graphics, anyway?"

He treated Carol to a long-suffering look. "Of course, but it'll be a dead end. There's no way Wellspring's going to be caught that easily."

As Anne handed around copies of the photograph, Denise said, "It was taken with a telephoto lens, almost certainly by someone in the crowd. The Great Hall was being evacuated, there were people milling about everywhere, lots had cameras."

The photo was a large black and white print. In the background a Family First sign, LESBIAN LOVER, was clearly visible. Marla Strickland, accompanied by Denise, was centered in the photo, her head turned in the direction of the camera. A neat red circle had been drawn over her face; a sticker at the bottom of the photo read, *This could be a rifle sight.*

Carol frowned at Marla, who was reflectively sloshing ice cubes in the bottom of a glass. "You left well before we started getting people out, so how come you're in the crowd?"

Denise made a face. "Sorry, Carol, it's my fault. Marla wouldn't budge until the evacuation was completed. I got her as far as the back door to the hall and she balked. My little lecture on the futility of being a dead hero didn't move her, so she waited until you were walking out of the building before she deigned to move."

"That was stupid," said Carol to Marla. "And you risked Denise's life as well as your own."

Marla shrugged. "What about yours?"

Sid laughed. "So we're all brave little soldiers . . ."

Carol wasn't amused. "Next time I expect you to do exactly what you're told when it's a security matter."

"Yes, ma'am!"

Reluctantly smiling at Marla's mock salute, Carol turned back to her copy of the photograph. "No fingerprints, of course."

Sid shook his head. "Nothing on the photo. And no joy with the paper the print was made on — it's standard stuff. And, other than Denise's fingerprints and those of the guard who found it, the box is clean and so is the note that came with it. All we know is that someone slipped the box under the dais some time after the hall was searched for bombs."

Marla came over to tap a fingernail on the front

page of the morning paper: UNI BOMB HOAX. "You're not mentioning the shoe box or the photo. Why?"

"Wellspring knows," said Carol, "and so do we. If it gets out in the media, we run the chance of a copycat hoax using the same methods. That would only confuse things."

"Whoever they are they *want* publicity about their beliefs," said Anne, "so I bet copies of this photo are on their way to the media right now."

Sid grinned at her. "I bet you're right."

Flicking the corner of the photograph, Marla said, "Could someone have shot me?"

"With great difficulty," said Sid. "It's all very well to wave a camera about, but a rifle with a telescopic sight would have excited some interest in the crowd."

"But the box could have been a bomb, couldn't it?"

"There'll be metal detectors on all entrances from now on, although it means you're going to get complaints because it means long lines while people wait to be checked."

"It could have been a bomb?" Marla repeated.

Sid nodded slowly. "Sure could have," he said.

Madeline answered the phone after the fifth ring. "Carol. I was hoping you'd call." Her tone was neutral.

"I'm flying to Brisbane later today. There are several appearances before we return to Sydney."

"Yes, I know. Our Queensland network is taping for my special on Marla."

Carol had rehearsed what she'd say, but found herself apologizing instead. "Madeline, I'm so sorry. I just walked out on you yesterday. I shouldn't have done that."

Madeline said ruefully, "My timing's always been so good before."

"It wasn't your timing. I just wasn't expecting . . ."

"Come on, Carol." Her tone was chiding. "You know I've never been indifferent to you."

Keeping her voice light, Carol said, "Did you intend it to be reciprocal?"

"Reciprocal?"

"The love. You said you wanted me to love you."

"You can take that for granted."

"I don't take anything for granted."

After a pause, Madeline said, "Carol, I've loved you for a long time. There just didn't seem any point in telling you so."

Madeline's candor killed the flippant remark Carol was about to make. She felt a confusion of feelings — caution, surprise, excitement. The silence stretched. At last Madeline said, "You're speechless, Carol? Surely not."

"I'll call you from Brisbane. Okay?"

"Please."

Carol put down the receiver and stood with her hand on it for a long time. She was tempted to call back, but what could she say that Madeline wanted to hear?

She started as the phone rang under her hand. It was Mark Bourke.

"What can I do for you, Mark?"

Bourke chuckled. "It's what I can do for *you,* Carol. You asked me to find out who might have used a little political pressure to have you appointed to guard everyone's favorite feminist."

"And?"

"And the fascinating thing is that I can't find out. Usually some little cog in the political machine will talk, but this time even my powers of persuasion have been stretched."

Carol smiled at his indignation. "It probably wouldn't make any difference if I knew, Mark, so don't worry about it."

"One name did turn up a couple of times, though I wouldn't give it too much weight."

"Who?"

"Richard Novell. He's a backbencher in the government and doesn't have a high profile."

Puzzled, Carol said, "I've heard the name, but I've never met him. I don't even know what he looks like, so why would he be interested in whether or not I was Strickland's bodyguard?"

"I can't imagine he would, since he's an old-fashioned right-wing conservative." He gave a vexed grunt. "Sorry I haven't come up with anything worthwhile."

"Mark, do me a favor. Keep plugging away. You might get something yet."

"Okay, Carol. And look after yourself."

After she broke the connection the warmth in his voice lingered, leaving her with an unexpected need for the familiar: the ordinary routine of her day; the blank beige walls of her office; the camaraderie of her peers. And for a time when her sexual identity had been entirely separate from her professional life.

Carol was looking forward to seeing Brisbane again, even though she wouldn't have much opportunity to appreciate its relaxed friendliness and balmy subtropical climate. She had fond memories of visiting friends there when she and Justin had been newly married. They'd stayed in a typical Queensland Colonial house, roofed with corrugated iron and built up on stilts to allow the air to circulate underneath. There were wide cool verandas and metal hoods over the windows. Carol had been fascinated by the interior painted wooden walls with the slats running vertically and the pressed metal ceilings from which broad-bladed fans were suspended.

Since Brisbane was only one and a half hours from Sydney by air, Carol arranged for their party to be booked, under pseudonyms, for several of the scheduled flights. They left the VIP lounge just before the flight Carol had selected was to leave the departure gate. Walking briskly down the slight incline to the plane, Carol realized how diminished Marla seemed in jeans and a T-shirt. With her dark hair tied back in a ponytail, she seemed so much younger and less formidable than her public image.

In the comfort of first class Marla and Anne Newsome sat together, Anne in the aisle seat to offer protection in the unlikely event that someone would attack while they were in the air. Behind them Gary slumped next to a white-faced Pam Boyle. Carol, who was across the aisle with Denise, leaned over to touch Pam's arm. "Are you okay?"

Pam slid a sideways look at her. "I don't like flying."

"You must do a lot of it with Marla."

"I do, but it doesn't mean I have to like it." She seemed to hear the curtness in her tone, because she said in a softer voice, "Thanks for asking. I'll be okay once we take off."

"Takeoff and landing are the most dangerous times," said Gary with gleeful malice. Pam shut her eyes.

Amused, Denise said to Carol, "What a total sweetheart that guy is."

Keeping her voice low, Carol said, "Have you found out what Gary meant when he told me he did special duties for Marla?"

"Think he was bullshitting, Carol. He's a failure from the word go. His father's a well-respected doctor, and expected his only son to follow in his footsteps, but no such luck. Gary either has no brains, or no application. Whichever, he didn't get the grades for medicine. That's why he's traipsing around with his stepmother. It gives the illusion he's useful for something."

"Gary speaks very well of you, too."

Denise grinned at Carol's mockery. "On that subject, I gather Pam Boyle objects to my sexuality."

"And mine. Who told you?"

"Gary. Who else? He likes to cause as much trouble as he can."

Carol glanced across to where he lounged in the window seat, gazing out the window and absently running a finger over his meager mustache. "Why would he bother?"

"Keeps him entertained, I suppose. He knows he can't be fired, whatever he does — there's no way Marla will complain to her husband about his son."

The plane had stopped its interminable taxiing and was quivering at the end of the runway while the captain requested cabin crew to be seated for takeoff. Carol wasn't soothed by his calm voice; she'd never been able to overcome the irrational belief that the plane needed her concentrated thought to make the transition from ground to air.

She waited until the usual miracle had been accomplished, the wheels had retracted with a satisfying hydraulic clunk, and they were safely heading north, then she continued their conversation. "Why wouldn't Marla complain about Gary? I've never seen her suffer in silence over anything else."

"I hear her marriage is a bit rocky."

"*That* isn't in the files."

Denise looked pleased with herself. "I have my sources."

"Okay, masterspy, tell me all about it."

"Dr. Roy Hawkins is her second husband and a successful pediatrician. He's a smooth operator with anxious parents, specifically the female ones. With Marla away so much, he has time to play. Nothing serious until last year, when there was a full-scale blowup over an affair he had with a rich lawyer's wife. Dr. Roy got it on both fronts — the woman's husband threatening bodily harm on one side and Marla raging on the other."

"No talk of divorce?"

"Seems to have been patched up, but who knows what's going on under the surface . . ."

Carol mentally reviewed the condensed information in the files she'd skimmed. "Didn't Roy Hawkins put money into Strickland Enterprises at the beginning?"

"He was every feminist's ideal husband, publicly supporting his wife's philosophy and putting his money where his mouth was. Now that the organization's self-supporting, both from contributions and royalties from Marla's books, he's taken a back seat. Maybe he's tired of being called Mr. Strickland."

"Would Marla's death be any advantage to her husband?"

Denise looked at her with mock horror. "Why Carol, you're not suggesting Dr. Hawkins is paying Wellspring to kill his wife, are you?"

"No. Just tossing ideas around."

Denise settled back in her seat. "If I may toss an idea of my own, we do have adjoining rooms in the hotel."

"And?" She raised an eyebrow.

"Anne Newsome will be on duty most nights in the hotel suite, since you'll be saving yourself for Marla's appearances. I'm just suggesting, when you have the chance, maybe you'd like to . . ." Denise grinned provocatively, ". . . relax."

"Thoughtful of you," said Carol wryly.

"And speaking of Anne, I think she might be sucked in by Sid Safer."

"How so?"

"He's got quite a rep as a performer, and being married doesn't slow him down one bit."

"Anne can look after herself." Carol looked along the aisle to where her young constable sat, wondering if Denise's speculation could be true.

"And watch out for Sid, yourself."

Carol gave her an incredulous smile. "I don't find him attractive."

Denise said soberly, "That's not what I mean. He's charming, but he's very conventional."

"Meaning?"

"You might win him over yet, Carol, but past history shows he's not all that keen on gays."

Carol was curious. "Has he caused trouble when you've worked with him before?"

Denise made a face. "The odd disparaging remark, but we weren't working closely together — it was just liaison on a couple of cases. Let's say I have some fairly serious reservations about Sid." She grinned. "I'm paid to be suspicious."

"How did you come to join ASIO?"

"You won't believe it, Carol, but I answered an advertisement."

"You're absolutely right. I don't believe you," Carol laughed.

Denise feigned offense at Carol's levity. "I'm telling the truth. I was in my early twenties, finishing an arts degree at the National University, and ASIO were in the midst of a rare recruitment drive. Since I had no idea what I was going to do for a crust and my parents were making strong 'get a job' noises, I applied, and, to my complete astonishment, I was accepted for training."

"You must have liked it — you're still there."

Her expression serious, Denise said, "Don't laugh at me, Carol, but I love the fact I'm working for my country. Do you understand that?"

Unexpectedly touched by her sincerity, Carol nodded. "I can't think of a better reason for staying in the job," she said.

CHAPTER NINE

The suite in the Brisbane hotel lacked a breathtaking view of a harbor like Sydney's, but it was comfortingly luxurious and looked out over city lights. Marla went to the window to gaze at the city. Leaning her forehead against the glass, she said, "Do I have to watch out for snipers?"

Her tone was light, but Carol could hear an undercurrent of stress. "You're okay. This suite's been chosen because there are no direct sightlines from other buildings." She didn't put her thoughts into words: *But if someone really wants to kill you,*

Marla, there's no guarantee that I, or anyone else, can stop it from happening.

The phone rang, and Bev Diaz came from the other room to answer it. "Who? No, there's no reason for him to see Marla."

Turning from the window, Marla said, "Who is it?"

"Hold on," Bev said to the caller. She looked tired and irritated. "Keil Huntling. He says he wants to see you personally."

"Where's his sister? The security arrangements were negotiated with *her*, not him." She frowned at Bev's don't-blame-me shrug. "It's your job to get answers," she said coldly. "I don't like surprises."

Bev's pale face reddened, but her expression didn't change, so Carol couldn't decide if it was anger or embarrassment.

"I'll get rid of him."

"No. Send him up."

Bev stared at her for a moment, then snapped into the phone, "Send Mr. Huntling up with one of his own guards."

Carol said mildly, "Why do you bother continuing with a private security firm? After that car bomb, you've got government coverage in spades."

"I've signed a contract with Cynthia Huntling and I'll honor it. And the company's been perfectly efficient, so far."

"We can't be absolutely sure one of Huntling's staff isn't a potential danger. They've been checked, but it's still a possibility."

There was a discreet knock. Automatically, Carol touched the gun in the holster under her loose shirt.

Marla raised a hand to halt Carol before she could open the door. "You've met Keil Huntling already?"

"Yes. Last Sunday."

"What do you think of him?"

"I'll let you form your own opinion . . . Come in, Mr. Huntling."

Keil Huntling looked past her to Marla. He was dapper in a dark suit, his face flushed and his pale blue eyes shining. "Ms. Strickland! I'm delighted to meet you. I believe you met Cynthia in the States, but I haven't had the pleasure . . ."

Tucking his flat maroon briefcase under his left arm, he advanced with right hand extended. Marla touched his meaty hand briefly. "I haven't met your sister, Mr. Huntling, although I've spoken to her on the phone. Pam Boyle on my staff did all the negotiations on my behalf."

Carol watched him closely. It was bizarre to think that the head of Marla's security firm might present a threat, but his visit seemed contrived and she neither liked nor trusted him. She said, "What are you here for, Mr. Huntling? All security matters for the tour are to be cleared through the Federal Police."

He smiled winningly at Marla, as though she had asked the question. "Actually, I'm here about the tour in general. I've all the details of each engagement, and I want to urge you to either increase your security substantially, or to curtail, or perhaps cancel —"

"No."

Marla's blunt interruption heightened his color. "Please. Hear me out."

"I have to change for tonight, Mr. Huntling, so please be brief." She sat down on the edge of a chair, her posture indicating it would be a temporary position.

"Regarding your MOWIG booking at the university, a courier delivered copies of the photograph and note this afternoon to our head office in Sydney."

Intending to puncture Huntling's cocky self-importance, Carol said, "Media outlets have had the same delivery. We know that. And the courier company was paid in cash by an anonymous woman, so there's no lead there."

"But *we* got an additional item." He made a ceremony out of unzipping his briefcase. "I'm sure Ms. Strickland would want to see it herself." He extracted a neat green plastic folder. "It was *this*," he said, handing it to her with a flourish.

"Has it been fingerprinted?" Carol said sharply.

He didn't bother to look at her. "You know there won't be any prints. Wellspring is too professional for that."

"You should have informed the Federal Police immediately."

Huntling waved away Carol's statement. "They can have it after Ms. Strickland sees it."

Marla opened the folder and Huntling leaned over to explain. "That's a floor plan of the Great Hall showing the location where the cardboard box was left, and indicating all the possible ways into the hall." He stabbed at the page with a thick forefinger. "And notice even the roof trapdoor and the under-floor access points are marked." He flipped over a page. "And here's the floor plan for tonight's appearance at the Suncorp Piazza. See, even the lighting catwalks have been drawn in." He turned another page. "And this is the Sydney Opera House main hall, where you're booked next weekend . . . and the last page . . ."

The final item in the folder was a photocopy, apparently from an article on assault weapons. There was an illustration for each one, and Carol recognized many: Uzi 9mm machine pistol; AK-47 semiautomatic rifle; Street Sweeper 12-gauge shotgun. Across the picture of the Colt AR-15 Sporter was printed in red: *Assassin's choice.*

Carol reached over and took the folder. "This should have been given to us straightaway."

"I was coming up to Brisbane to oversee our security anyway, so I thought I'd bring it myself . . ."

Smiling grimly, Carol said, "You know better than that."

He turned his attention to Marla. "Ms. Strickland — Marla — my company's only concern is your safety . . ."

Marla stood. "I'm sorry, Mr. Huntling, I do have to get ready. This is my assistant, Beverly Diaz. If you have anything further, please discuss it with her. Carol, can I see you for a moment?"

Carol, holding the green folder, followed her into the bedroom. Marla shut the door and turned to face her. "What do you think?"

"About the folder? Wellspring's trying to make you cancel — and maybe you should."

"I don't frighten that easy." She gave a small laugh. "Sounds heroic. The truth is that maybe I *do* frighten that easy, but I'm not going to cancel anything." She touched Carol's arm. "I'm relying on you to keep me alive."

Bev opened the door. "He's gone, but the s.o.b.'s staying in this hotel."

Carol privately agreed with Bev's assessment, but she asked neutrally, "Do you have any idea why Mr. Huntling is so keen to impress?"

"Sure." Bev's face twisted into a sneer. "The asshole is talking of expanding into North America, specializing in security for visiting Australian media and music personalities, and he thinks Marla's business in the States will help him. She's a high profile client who'll get Huntling's name known —" She was interrupted by the phone on the bedside table. Snatching it up, she barked, "Yes?" As she listened, her expression changed from scorn to angry concern. "You're kidding me!"

Slamming down the phone, she turned to Marla. "That was Pam. A fax has just come through from Connecticut. Dr. Lucas Britt has just announced a lightning tour of Australia. He's already on his way."

Marla sat on the edge of the bed. "Now, *there's* a genuine asshole," she said.

From a security viewpoint, Carol hadn't been happy at the choice of the Suncorp Piazza for Marla's Brisbane appearance. She'd spent the best part of the morning examining the auditorium and its sur-roundings. The Suncorp Piazza was within the South Bank Parklands on the shore of the Brisbane River, which had originally been the site of World Expo in the eighties. The whole area had been developed into a complex of paved walkways, formal gardens and attractions such as an artificial beach and a rainforest display. In addition a wide selection of restaurants drew crowds of people who walked along the river bank to admire the city lights or traveled by boat along an artificial canal. Any would-be assassin could melt into the crowds in order to escape by water or by way of the extensive carparks.

Marla was taken to the site in the early evening. She chatted to Carol as their security entourage made the short journey from the hotel along city streets and over the Victoria Bridge. But now, in the dressing room, Marla seemed much more apprehensive, sharing Carol's unease. She was pacing around, the make-up and full length mirrors reflecting her agitated movements. "You know, Carol, that dummy bomb at Sydney University really got to me. It could have so easily been real . . . This place has been checked out completely, hasn't it?"

"A specialist squad with sniffer dogs has just finished going over the whole building. Each entrance, including the loading dock, is guarded and everyone in the audience has to go through metal detectors before getting in."

She seemed reassured by Carol's business-like tone. Allowing Bev Diaz to seat her at the make-up mirror, she looked at Carol's reflection. "You'll be with me on the stage?"

"Absolutely. I'm one of the honored guests. Do you think I look the part?"

Marla turned to eye her neutral-toned suit and flat leather shoes. "You'd look better with some jewelry and higher heels."

"I just want to fade into the background." Carol didn't mention that she was wearing low heels so that nothing would impede her if she had to intercept a direct physical attack. Quite apart from Wellspring, the publicity given the bogus bomb scare in Sydney might be all the encouragement an unbalanced person needed to make a try for notoriety.

Anne put her head into the dressing room. "Sid wants to see you."

Carol beckoned her inside, then went out into the corridor, shutting the door behind her. The noise from the waiting audience filtered through the structure as a constant hum loud enough to make Sid raise his voice. "Everyone's in place. Denise is coordinating the perimeter and I'll be inside the auditorium, so if something happens, I'll be on the spot fast."

"I'll have Anne off to the side of the stage. I'm sitting with the VIPs."

"Where else?" he asked with mock surprise. "And by the way, I've sent the Huntling folder to the lab, but it's almost certainly a waste of time."

"Have you considered the possibility that Keil Huntling fabricated it himself, so he could have an excuse to promote himself to Marla?"

"You're not a trusting soul, Carol, but you could be right. I don't think it will help us one way or the other."

Anne came out of the dressing room, shutting the door behind her. "Who's Dr. Lucas Britt? Marla's frothing at the mouth about him. I've heard the name, but that's all."

Sid Safer grinned at her. "He's as far right as

you can get without falling off the edge. Got his degree by post from some mail-order university and started his own religion, the Church of God's Desire."

"Sounds a bit raunchy."

"Please! Only within the everlasting bonds of marriage." Sid's grin widened. "In case you want to know, according to Dr. Britt, God's Desire calls for every social advance in the past two hundred years to be abandoned. Personally, I think Britt's best line is, 'The Almighty has decreed everyone in his place, and a place for everyone.' Apparently wherever God puts you, you stay, so there's to be no equality for minorities or women."

"Surely no one takes him seriously," said Anne.

"Too right they do. He's got one of the fastest growing television ministries in the States. And one of his chief hates is feminism, so you can see why he'd love to bring Marla Strickland down."

Carol said, "Any link between the Church of God's Desire and Family First here?"

"Ah, Carol. You're always looking for links, but I have to disappoint you this time. Family First isn't *nearly* conservative enough for Dr. Britt. I mean, they allow women to *speak* in public, and that's a no-no for God's Desire. Women are to be silent because God has made them inferior to man. Lucky for you two I don't subscribe to that view." He looked at his watch. "Time to check the troops."

Watching him walk off with his long, loose-limbed stride, Anne said, "I like Sid."

Something in Anne's voice made Carol look at her sharply. "How much?"

She looked embarrassed. "He's separated from his wife . . ."

Carol was doing a rapid reshuffle of her preconceptions. Anne romantically involved? Carol hadn't really given much credence to Denise's comments about Sid Safer's conquests, but now she wondered if she hadn't been blind to what was happening. She knew from the grapevine that Anne had casually dated several young officers, but she'd always seemed essentially uninvolved and much more interested in her job and in sport than in relationships. "I had no idea things were serious between you."

"They're not," Anne said hastily. "At least, not yet ... We've only had a couple of drinks together ..."

Pam Boyle came striding down the corridor. Seeing Carol and Anne, she slowed, assuming her usual awkward stance. "Is Marla ready? She's already late and everyone's getting impatient."

An audience of over three thousand crammed the auditorium. The primal roar at Marla's entrance caught Carol's breath. She glanced at Marla's exultant face. To have that power to unite thousands in a single rush of shared emotion must be the ultimate high.

Tonight Carol was seated on the platform with the Brisbane feminist VIPs and political figures courting the women's vote. She was positioned at the end of the row to Marla's left. To the extreme right of the stage Anne stood unobtrusively.

Marla began to speak. Carol was accustomed to her commanding delivery, but tonight the American gave something extra. The air around her seemed to crackle with energy as she launched into her topic. "This is the Year of the Smear — the year of whisper campaigns against women elected to, or standing for office, the year of targeting women who oppose the ultra-right's warped vision of 'family values' . . ."

Sitting forward on her chair, feet positioned to propel her into quick response, Carol constantly checked the auditorium. The fan-shaped main area on the western side was divided into eight blocks of steeply inclined seating. If anyone was to use a high-powered rifle it would be from that elevation, so each of the eight blocks was under separate surveillance. To the extreme left and right of the stage were two smaller blocks of seating. Carol had wanted these kept empty because of the proximity to the stage, but had been overruled by Marla, who insisted that people who had bought tickets for this area had a right to sit there. Anne and one of Sid's officers had been designated to watch these two areas.

Carol's main interest was the floor of the arena, directly in front of the stage, where the configuration held six hundred. The television crew taping for *The Shipley Report* had been checked out; while she monitored their activities, she was more interested in the general audience. She was looking for anything unusual: someone suddenly standing, any gesture or movement that might indicate a threat. Although everyone had been through metal detectors, there were sophisticated ceramic and plastic weapons that wouldn't be picked up in mass screenings.

The stage had been the last area checked by the bomb squad, so she could ignore the skin-crawling thought that a bomb nestled below the speaker's desk ready to maim and kill.

One word brought her attention back to Marla. "Lesbian is an honorable word that some of our sisters are proud to bear — yet it is a fact of political life that, using the community's fear and ignorance, the radical right, in tacit conspiracy with all religions, will use this one word to smear a woman candidate. To support gay rights in any way is an invitation to start a rumor campaign. 'Family values' are used as a stick to beat anyone who dares to have enlightened views on social issues . . ."

The attack, when it came, was at first disguised by the standing ovation that greeted the end of Marla's speech. ". . . so I say to you, feminist-bashing will provoke a backlash of its own! Women will take their rightful place in the home, in government, in the judiciary, in the economy." She raised her arms in her characteristic gesture. "We *will* prevail!"

As those in the front row stood, clapping, there was a spontaneous movement towards the front. Carol's eyes focused on the young woman in jeans and a T-shirt just before she vaulted onto the stage with one athletic movement.

A surge of adrenaline drove Carol to her feet, her mind simultaneously assessing the nature of the threat. She was moving before it had registered: a truncheon; wooden; raised to strike at Marla's head. *No need for my gun.*

Her reaction was automatic, practiced: intercept to become the primary target; balance, knees bent; forearm block at attacker's wrist; follow through with a sharp chin jab; disarm; seize attacker's hand, force the arm straight and lock the elbow joint.

The woman fell to her knees as Carol applied pressure. "Down! I'll break your arm!"

Carol was suddenly aware of the pandemonium around her. Sid was beside her, handcuffing the prone figure, the official party were standing, staring, the audience was in an uproar of confusion. "Where's Marla?" she shouted above the noise.

"Anne's got her off the stage. She's okay."

"This could be a diversion. There might be another attack."

He gave her a quick grin. "I know. Denise has got it under control." He bent to haul the handcuffed woman to her feet. "You worry too much, Carol."

CHAPTER TEN

It was late when Carol finally got back to the hotel. She changed into a pale gray track suit and joined Anne, Marla, Pam and Gary watching the late news. Marla leaned over and squeezed her hand. "Thanks. It all happened so fast I'm still not sure what happened, but I know you stopped her, whoever she was."

Carol made a don't-worry-about-it gesture. "Where's Bev?" she asked, curious because she hadn't seen her since she'd helped Marla in the dressing room before the appearance.

"On the phone dealing with the media," said Gary, his eyes on the screen. "Hey, look. Here it is . . ."

The Shipley Report's crew had captured the whole incident and it was being lovingly replayed in slow motion with an enthusiastic voice over: ". . . as you see, if it hadn't been for the quick action of Detective Inspector Carol Ashton, the visiting American feminist could have been seriously hurt, if not killed . . ."

Carol sat down gingerly, the sharp pain beneath her ribs reminding her of the breathless weakness she'd fought to disguise after she'd got the woman down. She watched herself on the screen as though it were another blonde, efficient Carol — saw her intercept the attacker before there was any chance the upraised nightstick could strike Marla, saw the economy and speed with which the woman had been disarmed. Next time — Carol was sure there would be a next time — she might not be so effective.

"Neat," said Gary with open admiration. He looked at Carol. "Neat," he said again.

"It's not neat that it's on national television. Marla, I should be replaced as your bodyguard. There's no doubt that everybody would recognize me now, so, in the event of an attack, they'll neutralize me before they get to you."

Marla's expression was stubborn. "I don't want you replaced." Her voice was strained. "You can always put Anne in the front line — she isn't well-known — but I want you there too."

Pam shifted uneasily in her chair. She kept her head down, her undisciplined brush of hair hiding her face. "I think the Inspector's right. She should go." An angry exclamation from Marla made her look up.

"Marla, *you've* been trying to get rid of her from the beginning," she said resentfully, "so don't blame me for saying the same thing."

"I've changed my mind." Marla smiled briefly at Carol, then bit her lip. "I feel safer when you're around, Carol."

"Don't push your luck, Pammy," said Gary spitefully. "*You* might be the one to go."

"You wish!" There was more open aggression in Pam's voice and expression than Carol had seen before.

Before Gary could respond, Bev stalked from the bedroom and flung herself down on the couch. "I've told the hotel switch to hold calls." She looked meaningfully at Marla. "Whoever it is."

Carol took Anne aside to bring her up to date. "The woman gave her name quite freely — Freda Sandys. No police record, but she is a paid-up member of Family First. They've disowned her, of course, and I'm sure there'll be a statement tomorrow saying how shocked Family First is that violence has been used by one of their members. It could be a setup, but equally, she could have acted entirely on her own. The weapon — a heavy wooden truncheon — was in the bottom of her shoulder bag when she entered the hall. It belonged to her — she had a great uncle who was an air raid warden in London during World War Two. Apparently a nightstick was standard issue, and it's been passed down in the family."

"No doubt a God-fearing family," said Anne dryly.

"Did she expect to kill Marla with one blow? That's all she would have time for."

"Freda Sandys isn't very clear on what she hoped to accomplish, except that it would be, if I can quote her, 'a blow for God.' "

Anne shifted restlessly from foot to foot. "A loony, then?"

"Almost certainly. Let's hope she's one of a kind. Even so, I'm asking for a check to see how she got her front-row seat." Looking at the young constable's drawn expression, she added, "I'll sleep here, in the suite. You go to the room and have a stiff drink." Apart from the suite, the Strickland party had adjoining rooms on the same floor. Two were for Gary and Pam, and the third one Carol and Anne used alternately, depending on who was guarding Marla.

Anne hesitated, then said, "There's something wrong."

Carol rubbed her forehead. She felt tired and impatient. "What?"

Anne glanced to see if they could be overhead, then said, "Just after we got back to the suite, Marla had a long phone call. She took it in the bedroom, but I couldn't help hearing . . . Well, she had a violent argument with someone. It ended with her screaming into the phone. Then she didn't come out for a while, and when she did, she looked pretty upset."

"No idea who it was?"

"No." Anne looked troubled. "I suppose it's ridiculous, but it really got to me. I'm so used to Marla being in control, to see her like that . . ."

After she'd gone Carol sat quietly while Gary and Pam said good night and left for their rooms. Bev

119

Diaz, who was sharing the suite with Marla, gave Carol a calculating stare. "I'm going to bed. I can see you two want to talk."

"Do we want to talk?" said Marla, rubbing her eyes. She looked exhausted, and Carol felt momentarily sorry that she was going to take advantage of her fatigue.

"Just for a few moments."

"Did you like what I said about lesbians tonight?"

"I felt positively validated."

Marla grinned at her ironic tone. "Glad you appreciated it, since I put it in for you. Now, Carol, I'm so tired . . ."

"I won't be long. First, the woman who attacked you belongs to Family First. It looks like she acted alone and the organization had nothing to do with it. She's under arrest, of course, and I'm afraid you'll have to make a statement to the police tomorrow. Her name's Freda Sandys. Have you ever heard of her before?"

Marla rested her chin on her hand. "I'm sure I haven't."

"I'd like a check of your files in the States. Her name may turn up in your hate mail."

"Why did she do it?"

Long ago Carol had stopped being amazed at the motives that drove people to act. "She's obsessive — says her religious beliefs convinced her that it was God's will."

"I need to go to bed," Marla yawned.

Carol had to lock her jaws to prevent a reflexive yawn in return. She looked down at her hands, fiddled with her black opal ring. "When you came back to the hotel you had a phone call that distressed you." She looked up to be shocked by the grief on Marla's face. "I'm sorry . . ."

Marla looked at her numbly. "How can you end a relationship so that no one gets hurt?"

"I don't think you can." Carol could see Sybil's face, her eyes glinting with angry tears. "I think everyone gets hurt, one way or the other." *Now that you've gone, Sybil, I feel hollow and incomplete.*

An impatient sigh. "I just want it to be over so I can stop feeling this way."

Carol made her voice softly sympathetic. "Your husband?"

"When you stop trusting someone you love, if you've got any brains you stop caring as fast as you can." Her mouth turned down in a bitter line. "Don't you?"

"It's easier to say than do." As Carol mouthed the cliché, she acknowledged to herself that there was nothing new that anyone could say about love and loss. "Do you want to talk about it?"

Marla huddled back into the chair, crossing her arms protectively over her breasts. "There's nothing to say. Roy says we've drifted apart. He says he's spent our whole marriage making sacrifices for my career." She gave an angry snort. "It must be a matter of perspective — I'd have sworn it was *me* who made the sacrifices."

"Perhaps counseling . . . some sort of marriage guidance . . ." Carol winced to herself at the empty platitudes.

"When Roy had his last affair — the last one I know of — we went into therapy together for months." Her mouth twisted. "We agreed his unfaithfulness was a *good thing* . . ." Her sarcasm was

121

obvious, "... because it allowed us to air our real feelings and overcome the problems we'd hidden from each other." She glanced at Carol. "Ever seen a therapist?" She looked penitent. "Sorry, that was a bit personal ..."

"I had to see a trauma counselor while I was recovering from the gunshot." She couldn't help adding, "It's standard, now, in the Police Service." *I've got to stop making excuses. It's not a personal weakness to see a therapist.*

Marla leaned forward, obviously curious. "Was it any help — you going to counseling?"

"I didn't think so at the time."

"And now?"

"I'm not sure." As she spoke, Carol wondered if she was being totally honest. She'd gone to the counseling sessions because she had to, and had expected to discuss the shooting and, after getting that out of the way, to terminate the process. The unruffled woman therapist, however, seemed to have more interest in Carol's life than one specific incident. Carol had resisted this invasion of her privacy, deciding to talk about innocuous things. Strangely, though, once she began to talk, thoughts and feelings she didn't know she possessed came to light. It had been painful, but if she was fair, it had often also been enlightening.

"Have you ever noticed," said Marla acidly, "how therapists never say anything directly, but always ask you how you *feel* about things?"

"To know what you really feel," said Carol, standing to indicate the discussion was over, "is the hardest thing ..."

Marla looked up at her. "I know what I feel

122

about women's rights. That's all I'm really sure of at the moment."

Although she didn't want to prolong the conversation, curiosity made Carol ask, "What made you into an activist?"

Marla stood, so their eyes were almost on a level. "A gap in your research, Carol?" she said sardonically. "I would have thought you'd have known about my strict upbringing."

"Not really."

"You didn't know that my father was a fire and brimstone fundamentalist who bullied my mother into acquiescence and raised my two brothers to be replicas of himself?" Almost to herself, she added, "He was a tyrant."

Fascinated by the intensity of Marla's response, Carol said, "And you rebelled?"

"Rebelled?" Marla gave a short, angry laugh. "Of course I didn't. I grew up trying to please my father — trying to win his love and approval. It was only when I was older I realized it was a waste of time. Underneath all his pious language was a deep-seated fear and hatred of anything female."

Carol thought how lucky *she* had been to grow up with the love and support of a beloved father. She said, "What changed you?"

Marla had been staring past Carol as though her past were playing on a screen. The question brought her back. "A teacher. Her name was Evelyn Martin and she was far too radical and free-thinking for our small town. She only lasted a year at our school, but in that time I learned what the courage to think and act for yourself could mean." She smiled affectionately. "I do wish I could find Miss Martin again and tell her what she did for me, but I never knew where she went after the school board fired her."

She yawned widely. "Sorry. I'll have to go to bed." She paused at the bedroom door to add with a hint of mockery, "Next time, Carol, you can tell me *your* life story . . ."

Anne relieved her at eight the next morning. The night had been uneventful and Carol felt refreshed, even though she'd slept lightly. She went to their shared room to pamper herself with a long, hot shower followed by a leisurely room service breakfast. As Carol poured a second cup of black coffee, the television murmuring away in the dark teak cabinet caught her attention. ". . . and Reverend Smedley, speaking on behalf of Family First, issued a statement about the attack on American feminist, Marla Strickland last night . . ." After yet another showing of the attack, the Reverend Smedley appeared, his clear-rimmed glasses and clerical collar gleaming, to express shocked dismay at the actions of Freda Sandys, who, he emphasized, might claim to be a member of Family First, but was quite unknown to himself or any other member of the committee. He added smugly that Family First would be praying for Freda, of course, and, it went without saying, for the soul of Marla Strickland.

This was followed by the hyperactive woman on the morning team, who announced a station exclusive: "We'll be carrying details of Freda Sandys' application for bail, and then she appears, herself, on

Brisbane Tonight to tell her own story. Why did she attack the famous American feminist? See this exclusive interview at seven tonight!"

After the required clump of commercials, another glossy member of the morning team smiled from the screen. "And now we bring you part of a media conference with Dr. Lucas Britt, arch-foe of feminism, in Sydney after his early morning arrival from the States . . ."

Dr. Lucas Britt, white-haired, red-cheeked and broadly smiling, came into the press conference with the springy gait of a much younger man. He looked around approvingly as he seated himself. "It's so great that God's will has taken me to your beautiful, beautiful country . . ." His resonant voice had a slight southern accent and he spoke slowly, with great import.

A reporter called out a question about Marla Strickland and a look of sadness obliterated the beaming smile. "I so regret the path Marla has taken. She's turned her back on the Lord and made herself proud in her own error." His heavy white eyebrows emphasized his frown of anguish as he continued, "The Almighty loves Marla Strickland dearly, but He will judge her. His arm is swift in vengeance against those who lead the innocent into wrongdoing." There was a pause while Dr. Britt converted his expression to one of righteous condemnation. "My duty is to warn you, Marla Strickland! You have turned wife against husband, daughter against father. You have encouraged wicked discontent, so that many no longer know their rightful place in God's pattern of life. You have associated with loathsome sinners. It is God's desire, nay, *command* that you serve Him according to His will! Renounce evil and come to the Church of God's Desire, and I will absolve you in His name."

Carol thought it an offer Marla would be well able to resist. She studied the man's benign expression as the next question returned the sunny smile to his face. Could there be an association between his sudden decision to come to Australia and the violence, threatened and real, against Marla? Although his word choice was similar to Wellspring's, this was merely the diction of the fundamentalist, with no indication of any connection between the two.

Dr. Britt was making an all-encompassing gesture. "Y'all should know that the Church of God's Desire is to be established here, in your wonderful country. As I speak, negotiations are going ahead for the purchase of appropriate land, for God has commanded me to plant the seeds of peace and devotion in your excellent city, so that His church may grow strong and powerful in order to smite the forces of evil."

The phone rang. She pressed mute on the remote control, continuing to watch Dr. Britt's genial face. In her estimation he was certainly a ham, but perhaps something more sinister as well.

Aunt Sarah's cheerful voice boomed from the receiver. "Carol? Didn't want to disturb you last night, but I was *most* impressed with the way you dealt with that woman. They've shown it on every newscast. You made it look easy enough for me to do!"

"You'd probably do a better job than me."

"Feeling a bit down, are we, dear?"

Her aunt's gentle mockery always made her smile. "I haven't fended off a single attack this morning, and I'm feeling deprived."

"Well, I won't keep you, Carol. Just wanted you to know there was a long message from Sybil on the machine."

Is she coming home . . . or has she changed her mind about me joining her? Carol was surprised by the conflict these thoughts caused her. "I can call and get the machine to play back to me later — so just give me the gist of what she said."

"Sybil's met up with some friends she used to teach with years ago, and they're hiring a car together and driving around England for a couple of weeks while she has a break from her course. She wanted you to know she'd be out of contact, in case you were trying to get in touch." Aunt Sarah paused, then added, "She sounded really happy."

"Are you trying to make *me* feel bad?" Carol snapped.

"No, dear. I'm trying to make you feel less guilty . . . Always supposing that you do."

Denise came into Carol's room grinning cheerfully. She flung herself into a chair and put her sneakers up on the coffee table. "You haven't taken me up on my offer."

"What particular offer was that?"

Denise ran her fingers through her dark blonde curls. "Unbridled passion, Carol. That's what I was offering."

"Enticing," said Carol dryly, "but unfortunately I haven't had the time, and we have a full schedule today."

"Actually, that's why I'm here. Marla has media interviews as well as a luncheon hosted by local women's groups. I know she has to go out for the luncheon as well as to give her statement to the cops, but for security reasons I think her television interviews should be done here in the hotel, no matter how much the networks complain about the change. And the radio ones can be by phone. It sounded like a reasonable suggestion to me, but Bev Diaz is bucking. She says Marla has to look as though nothing can intimidate her, so hiding in the hotel is out. I'd like your support on this."

"What does Marla say? She should have the last word."

Denise got up in one lithe movement. "Come and see for yourself. Personally, I think she's scared as hell, but she's not going to admit it."

"Okay. I've got to make a couple of phone calls, and then I'll join you upstairs."

Denise stood, irresolute. "Carol . . ."

Carol grinned. "Not more unbridled passion?"

"It might be off the wall, but I wonder if Bev Diaz is deliberately putting Marla at risk by insisting she leave the hotel."

"Why would Bev do that?"

Denise raised both hands. "Search me — but she *is* a bit suss, isn't she?" Pausing with her hand on the doorknob, she added, "Maybe a closet Wellspringer?"

Carol was thoughtful as she dialed Madeline's number. She'd told Sid about her conversation with

Bev Diaz regarding Alcoholics Anonymous, and he'd agreed with her that, perfect though AA meetings might be for exchange of information, there was nothing to suggest Bev was using them for this purpose.

"Madeline, it's Carol."

"You don't have to announce yourself, I'd know your voice anywhere."

And *she* would always recognize Madeline's low, tawny tones.

"I won't say you were brave last night, Carol, because you'd dismiss it as your job, but that was a beautiful bit of work with Freda Sandys."

"And beautifully replayed ad infinitum on television."

"You think Wellspring doesn't already know what you look like? Carol, you're too alarmingly modest if you do."

"I want to know if that first whisper of Wellspring's name you got came through some connection with AA."

Madeline was businesslike. "Okay, I'll see what I can find out and get back to you."

Thinking how rarely Madeline showed surprise, whatever the comment or question, Carol said, "I'd like to get back to *you,* in person, as soon as we return to Sydney."

"That can be arranged."

"I wouldn't want to interrupt your schedule."

Madeline chuckled at her gentle sarcasm. "Carol, you're the top of my list, always." Her playful tone changed as she went on, "I'll be speaking with Marla Strickland in a few moments. I've been contacted by Dr. Lucas Britt himself. As well as appearing on my show tomorrow, he wants to issue a challenge for a television debate sometime next week. Think she'll go for it? It'll be a great opportunity . . ."

"It won't hurt your ratings either."

Madeline laughed aloud. "That's why I love you, Carol. You're so direct!"

CHAPTER ELEVEN

Carol, accompanied by Denise, took Marla down to police headquarters. Their car and the escort vehicle were both driven by Federal Police officers, each accompanied by a uniformed Huntling guard. Although Denise pointed out frequently that private security agents were more likely to get in the way than save Marla from an attack, Marla was adamant that they stay.

While Denise took Marla to give her statement, Carol sought out the officer who had booked Freda

Sandys. "I know I have no jurisdiction in Queensland, but I'd like to speak with her."

The overweight, graying sergeant gave her a tired grin. "Your Police Commissioner's already pulled the required strings. Anything, Inspector, is apparently to be yours."

The interview room was like so many that Carol had been in: grimy off-white walls, uncomfortable metal chairs, a scratched table that wobbled when leaned upon, a battered tin ashtray and air that smelled of the ghosts of countless cigarettes.

Freda Sandys sat with rigid posture, staring expressionlessly ahead. A female police officer with an equally blank face stood in one corner. Carol flicked on the audiotape and dictated particulars of those present and the date and time, noting that Freda Sandys had specifically waived her right to have a lawyer present.

Last night Carol had only had time for impressions: a young woman, tall, athletic build, hair flying, eyes wide, as, weapon upraised, she'd shouted something incoherent. This morning the same woman sat motionless, her long chestnut hair neatly arranged, her hands in her lap. Her fingernails were bitten to the quick. She had small brown eyes and a tight mouth and was dressed in the same T-shirt and jeans she had been wearing when arrested, although the laces had been removed from her sports shoes.

"Freda, my name is Inspector Carol Ashton of the New South Wales Police Service."

"I know who you are." Freda focused on her for the first time. "You hit me." She looked away.

Carol leaned back in the chair to present a more approachable persona. She was sure it would be fruitless to try scaring Freda with the weight of punishment a possible attempted murder charge might bring, so she said in a friendly tone, "I'm sorry if I hurt you, Freda, but it was my job." Repeating the young woman's name could help forge an ephemeral relationship during the interview to encourage her to talk.

"I don't have to say anything." The tone was uncompromising, but she flicked a quick glance at Carol, apparently to assess the impact of her statement.

"No, Freda, you don't. But I'm very interested to know why you wanted to hurt Marla Strickland. Would you mind telling me?"

"She's evil. And so are you."

The police psychiatrist who'd given her a cursory examination that morning had noted that Freda Sandys did not appear mentally ill, but possibly had a personality disorder, because she was exhibiting characteristics that were abnormally rigid and inflexible.

"Did you mean to kill Ms. Strickland, or just to hurt her?"

That got the young woman's full attention. She almost spat out the words, "I was to silence her. Jezebel!"

Carol wished she could be contemptuously amused by the biblical reference, but Freda Sandys was staring at her with such an air of righteous purpose that she felt a chill. "Why not leave her to God?" she asked in a tone of polite inquiry.

"I was fulfilling God's purpose."

"Who told you that, Freda?"

She lifted her chin proudly. "God told me."

Carol spread her hands. "Help me to understand, Freda. Did someone in Family First give God's command to you?"

Freda looked at her suspiciously. "What are you trying to make me say?"

"I want to know how you knew that God wanted you to go to the Suncorp Piazza last night."

"I knew." There was a smirk on her pale face. "I was chosen."

Carol smiled pleasantly. "You must have known for some time, since you had a front row ticket. Did someone get it for you, Freda?"

"It was nothing to do with Family First, if that's what you're trying to make me say."

Carol looked at her reflectively. "Then it must have been Wellspring."

"I want to go back to the cell." Freda Sandys stood, causing an involuntary movement from the officer. Carol remained sitting. In that moment she had seen what she hoped to see. A flash of triumph on Freda Sandys' face.

Marla had refused to reschedule her media interviews to the hotel conference room, so she had several appointments before the formal luncheon at a riverside restaurant. She stalked out of Police Headquarters and flung herself into the limousine's back seat. "Gary, did you call ahead and say we'd be late? I've no idea why giving a simple statement took so long."

Gary could hardly have seemed less interested. He continued flipping through a magazine as he said,

"Yeah, it's under control. They're waiting for us now."

Marla glowered at Carol, who was sitting opposite her. "Why did I have to make a statement to the police? I didn't really see anything — it was just a whole lot of confusion. And don't try to soothe me by saying it's just routine. That's what the cop kept saying."

"I won't try to soothe you."

Marla's face broke into a grin. "You're good for me, Carol. I can't push you around." Her smile faded. "You know Lucas Britt's challenged me to a TV debate?"

Carol looked past Marla to check that Denise in the second security car was following the limo. "Madeline Shipley mentioned it to me when I spoke to her this morning."

Marla folded her arms. "I don't feel inclined to give that Southern weasel a platform where he can spout his views."

Gary looked up from his reading. "He'll spout them anyway, Marla, so why give him a chance to say you're a coward because you won't face him?"

Disregarding his comment, Marla said to Carol, "Lucas Britt is mighty good on a television screen. Have you seen him?"

"Only the press conference this morning."

"Then you'll know what I mean. He looks such a kind, benign old Southern gentleman, people don't notice the poison he's spewing out."

Surprised at Marla's reluctance to debate — Carol had been sure she'd leap at the chance — she said bracingly, "I'd back you ahead of him any day."

"So you think I should do it?"

"It's up to you."

"*I* think you should," said Gary. "Otherwise he'll say you're chicken."

"I don't give a damn what Lucas Britt says."

Gary put down his magazine. "You know, Marla," he said, "If you ask me, I think you're losing it . . ."

Carol stared at him. *Why are you trying so hard to get Marla locked into this television debate?*

The interviews went without incident, except for a small group of Family First protesters at each site. Carol and Marla changed vehicles with Denise, so that she went in the limo as a decoy and they traveled in an anonymous sedan to the luncheon sponsored by combined women's groups.

The restaurant with its white and silver facade was bankside, and the green water of the Brisbane River slid past its picture windows. The day was beautiful, warm and sunny, and Sid Safer, who'd met them at the restaurant, beckoned Carol outside once lunch was over and Marla had begun her speech.

"I've got three operatives seated in the crowd doing their best to look like radical feminists, and Denise and your Anne Newsome can keep an eye on Strickland."

The mention of Anne reminded Carol of her concern about the young constable and Sid Safer. Whatever he'd said to Anne, Carol hadn't heard that he'd separated from his wife. She wouldn't usually have even considered interfering, but she knew Anne looked up to her as a mentor, and she couldn't decide what to do about the matter.

The restaurant had been closed to the public for the function, so Carol followed Sid through the deserted outdoor dining area with its glass tables and bright umbrellas to a spot near the water. There a wharf jutted into the river, guarded by one of Sid's men.

Sid turned the chairs and positioned the umbrella so they had a clear view back to the indoor restaurant. "We're out of earshot here, but we can see if anything happens." He took out dark glasses and polished them. Putting them on, he said, "Okay, Carol, what's up?"

"I interviewed Freda Sandys this morning. She's playing the role of an unbalanced young woman who has a bee in her bonnet about feminism and specifically, Marla Strickland, but I don't buy it."

"I've tried checking how she could have been sure to get the front row position, but it's no go. Tickets for the auditorium were allocated in blocks and sold from several outlets. There's no way to tell if she bought it herself or someone did it for her."

Carol gazed at a yacht bucking gently at its mooring as a launch motored by. "I don't think we'll find evidence to prove it, but I'm sure Freda Sandys is part of Wellspring's campaign."

"Which is to get Marla Strickland."

"Not exactly. Everything Wellspring's doing is for publicity. They don't want to kill Marla, they want to use her to get media exposure for their views."

Sid stretched out his long legs and rubbed his face wearily. "I'm beat. Battling the religious right is hard work."

"Wellspring isn't the religious right, though I think they're allied with the movement. I'm beginning to think they are a lot more political than that."

"Everyone has a political angle these days . . . it's the only way to get anywhere."

"What if Wellspring is the extremist wing of a political group? There's plenty of precedents, for example Northern Ireland or the Middle East. Their candidates for political positions are apparently moderate, compared to the extremist groups who secretly support them."

"My dear Carol, you're getting paranoid. Next you'll be telling me there's a plan to take over the Australian government . . ."

She was irritated by his superior tone. "Not take it over — gain power. What do you think drives politicians to try for office when the general public regards them as lower than someone selling used cars? It's power . . . And power's said to be the ultimate aphrodisiac."

He put his hands behind his head. "Then I could do with some power in my love life . . ."

Carol spoke before she had time to think. "Anne works with me. I like and respect her. I wouldn't want her to be messed around."

Sid straightened in the chair. Taking off his dark glasses, he said, "Are you lecturing me, Carol? I could say it's none of your business."

She was angry to have so impulsively put herself in an embarrassing position. "Perhaps it isn't —"

She broke off as Bev Diaz approached. Her steel-gray hair was brushed severely back from her face and she wore an ill-fitting beige suit. Without ceremony, she pulled out a white metal chair and sat down. Leaning forward, she was about to speak when

Carol preempted her. "Bev, are free tickets given out for Marla's appearances? I'm thinking of seats for leaders of women's organizations or those who give substantial financial support."

Obviously impatient with the question, Bev said dismissively, "Naturally there are complimentary tickets. It's standard practice."

"Are they for specific seats?"

"Of course — do you think VIPs like sitting at the back? They want to be seen."

"Who's responsible for the distribution of these tickets?"

"Basically it's done from our head office in Connecticut, but any of us can request complimentary tickets if we want to." It was obvious the subject was of no interest to her.

"Did anyone request them?" Carol persisted.

"Not that I can remember. Why?"

Sid broke in with a lazy smile. "Well, you see, Bev, we're wondering how Freda Sandys got her front row seat."

"Through a booking agency, like everyone else. It couldn't have been a complimentary ticket, if that's what you're thinking — in the auditorium last night they were only to the left and right of the stage." She gave him a grim smile. "Sorry to disappoint you." Turning to Carol, she went on, "I've got something much more important to discuss. Marla told me during lunch that she's decided to go ahead with the debate. You know Madeline Shipley personally. Will she give us an edge against Britt?"

"I'm sure she doesn't agree with most, if any, of the things Lucas Britt stands for, but I don't think she'll favor Marla, if that's what you're asking."

Bev's dark eyes flashed. "Why not? Do you think that asshole Britt plays fair? And why doesn't Shipley support women? She should do everything she can to bring the s.o.b. down."

"Madeline's there to moderate the debate. Taking sides isn't her job," said Carol blandly.

Bev was impatient. "It's *everyone's* job! Otherwise that lying bastard gets away with it!"

"The world's full of lying bastards," said Sid amiably. "There's no point in lashing yourself into a fury over every one of them. Besides, Lucas Britt's so far off the planet no one with any brains would pay attention to what he says."

"Intelligence isn't a protection when people are looking for excuses! Why do you think Britt heads one of the richest sects in the States?" She slapped her hand on the table. "Because he tells people what they want to hear — that nothing's their fault. They don't have to take responsibility for themselves. All they have to do is destroy anyone who doesn't agree with what Britt says, and heaven on earth's guaranteed."

Sid cocked his head. "But isn't that what Marla Strickland is doing? Telling women it isn't their fault? That everything will be all right if the opposition's destroyed?"

Bev swept him with one long contemptuous look. "I'm fast coming to the view," she said, "that males should be killed at birth."

Watching her retreating figure, Sid said to Carol, "I *do* like playing devil's advocate . . ."

"Fine, but just don't play devil," said Carol.

CHAPTER TWELVE

The last appointment was a late afternoon television interview to be taped for a local news magazine program. Outside in the roadway five placard-bearing protesters waited patiently. As the cars swept up to the entry boom gates, one rushed forward to wave, STRICKLAND WILL BURN IN HELL.

"How in the hell did they know I'd be here?" snapped Marla.

"Who cares?" said Gary. He punched the controls of the electric window. "Get a life!" he yelled.

Furious, Carol shoved him back against the seat. "You've been told not to open the windows. You just put Marla at risk by doing that."

He wriggled under her restraining hand. "They're just a bunch of assholes with signs . . ."

"One of them could have had a weapon."

"Yeah, all right," he said sulkily. "I'm sorry."

Leaving Denise guarding the cars, Carol hurried Marla into the station. Gary grumbled as he trailed after them carrying Marla's large makeup case, "Why do you insist on having your own makeup? Studios supply the same stuff . . ."

Carol would have cheerfully backhanded him, but Marla shrugged off his petulance. "I know what makes me look good, I can't rely on any studio makeup artist getting the same effect."

When the glossy executive assistant had taken them to makeup, Marla went to the washroom. While she was absent Carol snapped open the clips of the makeup kit and began to go through the contents. She didn't really expect to find anything lethal, but she was curious to see if there was room to conceal a weapon. Gary watched her with a disdainful smile. "Think someone's spiked the lipstick with contact poison?" he asked. "Or maybe the tube's really a miniature grenade."

She gave him a level look. "It's not likely, because it wouldn't be public enough."

"What's it matter, if they want to get Marla?"

"Wellspring wants the maximum publicity — something that will get national attention."

"Yeah? As far as I'm concerned, it'd only be big news if it made the television networks in the States. Who cares what happens here?"

Carol looked at him thoughtfully. "You might have a point, Gary."

He seemed disconcerted by her approval. "Oh, yeah?" He pushed back the hair flopping over his forehead. "You think so?"

"You're keen to have your stepmother debate Dr. Lucas Britt, aren't you?"

"I guess." Her emphasis on his exact relationship with Marla irritated him, as she knew it would.

"And they've never appeared together before?"

"So?"

"It's my impression that in America Lucas Britt has as high a media profile as Marla, so I imagine television networks will show at least part of the debate."

Marla swept in to catch her last words. "I should hope so! I want to nail him in front of the biggest audience possible."

"Just so long as he doesn't nail *you*," said Gary.

The interviewer was a facile young man nattily dressed in a navy jacket, his very white teeth nicely contrasting with his deep tan. He'd done his homework, and seemed quite familiar with the main themes of Marla's campaign, running over the range of questions he'd be asking without a single impatient explosion from his guest, who, Carol thought, could eat most interviewers for breakfast.

Even though he was thoroughly professional, Marla was edgy, tapping her fingernails against the black leather folder she always took with her for interviews. Curious, Carol had flicked through it before an earlier interview, and Marla had explained how she always liked to have statistics and tables with her so that she would always have back-up if challenged or if she needed to amplify a point. "It's my security blanket," she'd explained.

Rather than share studio space with Carol, Gary had disappeared into the control room, where she could see him lounging, bored, against the wall. She'd noticed that over the past days he'd become more belligerent towards his stepmother, and Carol wondered how long it would be before Marla slapped him down. *He's acting almost as though he won't have to please Marla for much longer . . .*

The interview went smoothly. Carol was adept at handling the media herself, and her admiration for Marla had grown as she'd realized what a skilled performer she was. Warm, confident, at ease with the camera, never avoiding difficult questions, she gave answers that steered the interviewer in the direction she wanted to go. Her energy crackled through the screen and gave her words weight.

When the interview was obviously winding up, she broke in to face the camera directly: "As you may have heard, Dr. Lucas Britt, who heads a cult in America — the Church of God's Desire — is in Australia for a sudden, lightning tour that coincides with mine." Her tone implied this was not an accident. "And he has issued what he calls a challenge — a nationally televised debate." Her face was lit with an assured smile. "I'm delighted at last to have the opportunity, on *The Shipley Report* next Wednesday, to expose Dr. Britt's religious anti-woman ideas for what they are — gibberish."

* * * * *

When they returned to the hotel suite, Bev was waiting with an air of pleased accomplishment. "I contacted Madeline Shipley in Sydney and she arranged for her network station here to send over an unedited tape of Lucas Britt's media conference."

"Great." Marla didn't sound enthusiastic.

"You need to know everything he's said in public, Marla. He'll probably repeat half of it in the debate."

"How did you know Marla had agreed to do it?"

Bev gave Carol a pitying look. "If you knew Marla like I do, you'd realize she never backs down from a challenge, especially when it involves a target like Britt and his fascist church."

Smiling a little at Bev's endorsement, Marla said to Carol, "Come and watch it with me, Carol, you might have some ideas about how to counter the bastard." She raised her voice to call out, "And you too, Pam. You need to see this too."

Carol watched Pam as she sidled through the doorway, her shoulders characteristically hunched. *Are you really so awkward and introverted? Or are you playing a role — and laughing at us all?*

Denise followed Pam into the room. "I can tell you exactly what he's going to say. All these fundamentalist sects use the same script."

Bev waited until Marla had curled up on the end of the sofa. "Ready?"

The video began with the general confusion before the media conference began, then the hasty positioning of microphones as Dr. Britt settled himself into the chair behind the long table. Carol's mind

145

wandered: she'd already seen most of this on the morning newscast. She looked up as she registered that she was hearing something new.

"By their fruits ye shall know them," Lucas Britt intoned. He managed an expression that successfully combined regret and outrage. "And Marla Strickland is constantly in the company of those who are an abomination before the Lord." Pause for effect. "Women who love women ... men who love men."

"We'll get the cast-into-hell bit next," said Denise, who was sitting on the floor with her back against the sofa.

Solemnly, Britt continued, "They shall be judged and God will condemn them to the everlasting fires of hell."

"Close!" laughed Denise, ignoring Bev's frown at her interruption.

Pam Boyle looked down from her lounge chair. "Why does it amuse you to mock Dr. Britt? Many people believe what he says is true."

"Do you?"

"Of course not, but he *is* an extraordinary person. I think it would be a mistake to underestimate him."

"Yeah? He seems like a fairly standard bigot to me."

"Yes, he would ..." It was obvious that Denise's lack of insight was no surprise to Pam.

"You can argue outside," said Bev, turning up the volume, "Marla needs to hear this."

Carol noticed that Marla seemed more interested in the conflict between Pam and Denise than the television screen.

Denise said challengingly, "Whatever else, you *do*

believe what he says about homosexuality, don't you, Pam?"

Her mouth tightened. "Yes, I do. I know that homosexuality is wrong. It's not natural. But that's my personal opinion, and I don't imagine it worries you what I think."

"It worries me that apparently intelligent people can be so judgmental about lifestyles that don't match their own."

Pam uncoiled herself from her chair. She glared down from her full height, her voice vibrating with anger as she said, "It's disgusting and dirty."

Denise smiled up at her. "You're protesting so much, I'm beginning to wonder about you, Pam. If you're attracted to women, don't fight it. You'll find it's fun."

Later, while Marla was at the bar making herself a vodka and tonic and Carol was sipping mineral water, Carol said obliquely, "Gary didn't seem very happy today . . ."

Marla poured a slug of Smirnoff into a tall glass. "You mean, why do I put up with him being a rude horse's ass, don't you?"

"Why do you?"

She added tonic to her glass and slid onto the bar stool next to Carol. "I understand why he's acting that way, so most of the time I just ignore it."

Carol raised an eyebrow, but made no comment. Marla looked at her sideways with a small smile. "You're thinking how uncharacteristically sweet-natured I am? But you haven't seen Gary with his father. Roy expected his son to follow in his footsteps and become a doctor. When Gary flunked medical school, Roy didn't bother to hide his disappointment, and when Gary didn't come up with some other acceptable career option, my husband virtually washed his hands of him." She took a long swallow of her drink. "Gary isn't very mature and he idolizes his father, so of course he resents being packed off with me to fetch and carry. In his position I'd probably feel the same."

Carol gave a noncommittal, "Hmmm . . ." *Does Gary resent you enough to wish you harm?*

"Anything new on Wellspring?" said Marla, closing the topic of her stepson.

"No, but I have this feeling that Wellspring has a connection to the United States."

"You could be right — Lucas Britt turning up out of the blue seems more than a coincidence."

Carol looked into her glass, wishing it contained whiskey. "We've had briefings from both the FBI and the CIA. Britt looks clean and so does his organization. Extremely right of center, true, but innocent of wrongdoing. And I don't believe a word of it."

Marla rubbed her eyes. "I just want to get through this tour . . ."

"How long has Pam Boyle been with you?"

"I don't know . . . a year? She was big in direct mail campaigns when I recruited her, and she's really built up the Strickland Enterprises contributors."

"So what do you know about her?"

"Know?" Marla was obviously annoyed. "All I need to know — she's a dedicated feminist."

"And Bev Diaz."

"She's been with me for two years. I don't know how I coped without her management skills."

"She told you she was an alcoholic?"

Marla's mouth turned down. "Bev told me she was a *recovered* alcoholic. I don't see why you're hounding her about this — it's a disease, Carol, not a moral failing." She gestured impatiently. "You'll be asking me about Gary next."

"Actually, I was intending to —"

"Don't bother!" Marla snapped. "Whoever Wellspring might be, it's outside my organization."

"I'm sure you're right, but maybe you have ..." Carol paused, not sure of the word.

"What?"

"... a fellow traveler," said Carol.

"Don't be ridiculous," Marla said, finishing her drink as she had finished the subject.

Anne came up to relieve Carol for the evening. "Before you go, I'd like to tell you something."

Carol paused, intrigued by Anne's obvious unease. Anne cleared her throat. "It's about Sid ..."

"He's told you I said something to him. I'm sorry, Anne. As he pointed out, it's none of my business."

"Actually, I wish you'd said something to *me*." She rubbed her cheeks. "This is so embarrassing. I've been so stupid."

Wanting to help her, Carol said, "Forget it. It's nothing to do with me."

"No, I need to tell you. And it *is* something to do with you. Sid told me he was separated from his wife, but I began to wonder if that was true. Today, when I asked him pointblank, he was furious. He said he knew you'd told me to ask. When I said that wasn't the case, he ..." She gave a helpless gesture.

Carol wondered for one angry moment if Sid had hit her, but Anne seemed more shamefaced than distressed. "Sid did what?" she asked.

"He said, to quote him, that you were a bloody dyke who hated men. Then he told me to look out, or you'd put the hard word on me."

Controlling her rage, Carol said, "What did you say?"

Anne gave a small smile. "I told him where he got off ... And that I couldn't imagine how I'd ever been dumb enough to think he was attractive."

"Thanks for telling me."

"I thought you should know he might be saying things behind your back."

"I'll deal with it, Anne, but we're not going to mention it again, okay?"

That smug bastard, she seethed.

CHAPTER THIRTEEN

Carol called Madeline as soon as she got home. "I've just got back from Brisbane and I'm about to get into a shower."

"That's an alluring picture. Want me to come right over?"

Carol looked at Aunt Sarah, who was exuberantly clashing saucepans in the kitchen. "No, my aunt's here and she's insisting I need something to eat. From past experience I know it's hopeless trying to dissuade her."

"So I won't see you this evening?" Madeline sounded disappointed.

Carol smiled to herself. "Are you planning to go to bed early?" she inquired.

"Only if you're with me."

The lazy drawl made Carol tingle. "I don't imagine I'll be very long."

Madeline laughed softly, then said, "And Carol, so business won't intrude on pleasure when I see you later this evening, here's the answer to your question about Wellspring and AA — there's no connection that I can find. My informant tells me the first mention of Wellspring seems to have been in a homophobic group associated with fundamentalists, but I can't get any hard facts."

Carol was thoughtful as she picked up Jeffrey for a cuddle. She walked into the kitchen with Jeffrey draped over her shoulder, his purring an ecstasy next to her ear. "I'm going out after dinner."

"Madeline Shipley?"

"Yes."

Her aunt made a speculative face. "Sure what you're doing?"

"I'm not doing anything."

"I get the impression that if Madeline Shipley wants something, she gets it."

Jeffrey reproached Carol as she put him down on the floor. "So do I."

Aunt Sarah slapped down a couple of plates. "Don't fool yourself, dear. You've never been sure what you really want."

* * * * *

152

Madeline popped the cork from the bottle of Dom Perignon. She poured the champagne into two crystal glasses. "It's vintage, Carol. I hope you're impressed."

"I am, but why the expense?"

Madeline grinned. "I don't expect to seduce you with a cheap sparkling wine."

"You shouldn't expect to seduce me at all." When Madeline grew suddenly somber, she added, "I mean, it isn't necessary. I don't have to be persuaded."

"This is a change — has something happened?"

"That's uncharacteristically modest of you, Madeline. It's *you* of course."

Madeline picked up her glass. "A toast, but *you* make it."

Carol watched the bubbles rise and burst. "Do you want me to drink to us?"

"Us? There isn't an us. It's just you and me."

Carol suddenly wanted something more, something permanent. "Madeline . . ."

"What?"

"I want you."

Madeline laughed softly. "Not exactly all I hoped to hear, but it'll do."

Her mouth was warm, her hands firm in the small of Carol's back. Hungry — ravenous — Carol kissed her passionately. Madeline responded, then drew away. Too far on the dizzy climb to go back, Carol tightened her arms until Madeline was tight against the heat of her body. "You know how I feel, so don't tease me."

"Then don't tease *me*."

Her hard tone opened Carol's eyes. "What do you mean?"

"I feel too much for you. I don't mean to, and if I had a choice, I wouldn't, because, at the risk of sounding impossibly schmaltzy, I suspect you're going to break my heart."

Carol shook her head, passion and indignation warring. "That's unfair."

"You've always got Sybil in the wings, ready to wheel out if things get too serious."

"No." But she knew there was some truth in Madeline's harsh words. At some level Sybil *was* a safety net. She could escape by saying, "I'm sorry, but I really love Sybil . . ."

She didn't want to consider that. Bending her head, she kissed Madeline slowly, deeply, the thud of her pulse driving away thought. Madeline purred against her lips, "I need you now. I can't wait."

The almost unbearable rush of physical sensation centered in a spreading ache that cascaded heat down her thighs. Madeline was sliding her hands under her T-shirt, reaching for the catch on her bra, making her grow tighter, tighter. But this time she was going to be in control. "I want your clothes off — now!" she commanded.

Madeline chuckled against her throat, "I love a masterful woman, but you'll have to persuade me . . ."

"Take them off, Madeline. I don't want to tear anything."

"Are you really so impatient?"

"Yes!"

Madeline continued to nuzzle Carol's neck as she obediently slipped off her jacket and began to unbutton her blouse. "Will you help me?"

Carol laughed through her breathlessness. "I'll have to — you're too slow."

Naked, she scorched Carol's hands. "Your turn," she said, unzipping Carol's jeans. Carol wanted to prolong this luscious discomfort but she was lost as they slid together to the floor. Madeline was touching her as she needed to be touched, holding her as she needed to be held. She was throbbing, bursting. "Madeline!"

She groaned with the delicious lassitude that followed. Turning in Madeline's arms, she whispered, "I could love you . . ."

CHAPTER FOURTEEN

Before the morning meeting, Carol took Sid aside.
"I don't appreciate what you've been saying about
me."

He looked puzzled. "Saying?"

"Don't bother playing dumb, Sid. I've spoken to
Anne."

"Oh." He nodded sagely. "I'm afraid she might
have got the wrong idea, when I was just being
friendly . . ."

"I don't think she had the wrong idea."

His mouth tightened. "I hope you don't believe everything she says."

Carol didn't reply. She knew some of the contempt she felt must show on her face. At last he said, "So I might have shot my mouth off a bit — there's no harm done."

"Who else have you told your opinions on my sexual activities?"

He reddened slightly. "Look, if you can't take a joke —"

"A bloody dyke who hates men. That's supposed to be funny, is it? And the part I find particularly charming is the comment that I might use my position to force Anne to have sex with me."

His color increased. He smoothed back his blond hair, then straightened his tie. When he spoke, his usual insouciant manner was in place. "I just don't get it, Carol. I mean, you've got a son, and it isn't as if you couldn't get a man . . . Let's face it, you're bloody good-looking."

Carol narrowed her eyes. She said calmly, but with steely intent, "I'm not going to waste my time explaining anything to you, Sid, but I *am* going to make you a promise. If I hear that you've said anything like this again in public, I'll crucify you. I won't hesitate to go to your superiors. And I won't hesitate to take you in front of a tribunal."

His mouth twisted with bravado. "You couldn't take the heat."

"Don't rely on me keeping quiet, Sid. I've nothing to lose by going public. You have."

He tried a confiding smile. "Carol, I do think we've had a misunderstanding . . ." He spread his hands. "Let's forget it, eh?"

"They're waiting for us," she said.

Sid followed her to the other side of the room where papers and coffee mugs already littered the table. Denise handed Carol a coffee as she sat down. "Did you know your favorite politician is an honored guest *again*?"

"Who? Marjory Quince?"

"Nope. The man who would be our next Prime Minister — Joseph Marin himself."

Anne looked up. "He hasn't got a chance."

"Don't be so sure. He's gathered quite a little group around him and he's quietly getting the numbers from the conservative wing of the party for a challenge. It won't happen this year, but if our present leader keeps on his unpopular ways, I'd bet on next year some time."

Bev Diaz rustled her papers. "Look, can we get on with a review of the security arrangements?"

Carol steepled her hands. "Denise, has Joseph Marin got a key numbers man to marshal the votes for him?"

"He certainly does, but you probably won't have heard of him."

"It wouldn't be Richard Novell, would it?"

Denise looked at her in admiration. "Well, you *are* a detective, Carol! You're absolutely right."

Mark Bourke was apologetic. "Carol, I've tried, but I keep getting a brick wall. I'd bet my last dollar that Richard Novell is involved in some way, but whatever political influence was used, a very effective smokescreen's up. All I can be sure of is that Marjory Quince was very reluctant to appoint you, but she was heavily persuaded, and she instructed the Commissioner to go ahead, even though he shared her misgivings that you weren't fit enough."

"And the persuasion came from Federal government circles?"

"Yes. Definitely from Canberra."

"I think I'm there to discredit Marla because I'm a lesbian. Lucas Britt is having a field day on the subject."

"People like him always have a go at gays. It's an automatic target."

"Mark, I want you to do something else for me. I need to know where Cynthia Huntling is. She's the head of the security firm Strickland Enterprises hired to protect Marla, but she's elusive as a ghost. I've seen her brother, but I'm beginning to wonder if she really exists."

"Piece of cake." Bourke sounded cheerful at being given an attainable task. "Anything else?"

"You remember the bombing of the women's clinic in Paddington last year? The one that Family First was picketing every day because abortions were carried out on the premises."

"Sure. We never nailed anyone for it."

"Will you dig up the file, Mark? I'd like a list of anyone who was considered as being a possible suspect at the time."

"You got it. That all?"

"Yes, but I'd like it fast."

"I'll get back to you, but in the meantime, look after yourself, Carol."

Carol felt a twinge in her side. "I'm trying," she said.

Carol, Anne and Marla left for the Sydney Opera House in the late afternoon, although Marla wouldn't appear on the stage of the Concert Hall until eight. When she protested at leaving the comfort of the hotel early, Carol was firm: "I want you safely in the complex before anyone could expect you to arrive, because the word on the street is that there could be some fairly strong protests against you this evening."

Marla, Anne and Carol were in a white limousine with a Huntling security guard and a Federal Police driver, while Denise rode shotgun in an unremarkable blue sedan with heavily tinted windows. Bev, Pam and Gary were scheduled to join them later.

There was a short drive along Circular Quay where busy ferries docked and departed constantly, then they turned onto Bennalong Point. Only designated vehicles were allowed through, and the guard checked their credentials carefully before waving them on.

The gigantic vaulted shells that formed the Opera House floated against a deep blue sky. Sydney Harbour, green-blue, lapped at the granite boardwalk that surrounded it on three sides. On the fourth side the green abundance of the Royal Botanic Gardens gazed down from a low sandstone cliff.

"Wow," said Marla, "what a great building, but I don't have to walk up all those steps, do I?"

Carol smiled as she looked at the massive flight of

wide terraced steps that ascended to a glass wall contained within the parabola of the first shell. "You can if you like, but I *was* intending to take you through the stage door that's in a tunnel running under those steps."

The limo went from dazzling light into comparative darkness as they drove into the passageway and drew up at the ground floor entrance. Carol felt happier once she had Marla past the stage door security and into the maze of passageways that held the dressing rooms, but Marla had a complaint. "Don't I get to look around the Opera House? At the very least I need to see the Concert Hall where I'll be appearing."

"Anne will take you to the Green Room if you want something to eat, because it's restricted entry, but I want to personally check everything out before you try a tourist tour. Okay?"

Marla looked mutinously through the narrow dressing room window at the scintillating surface of the harbor, then she grinned at Carol. "It's hell being a celebrity."

Carol thought about Marla's flippant comment as she closed the cream-colored dressing room door behind her. So many people envied the famous and wanted to change places with them. But there was a downside to everything. Carol's own high media profile was both a blessing and a curse. She could expect favors regarding access to people and the provision of information, but she also endured public scrutiny, and the revelation that she was a lesbian had exposed her to criticism and comment in the media. True, she'd gained support, often in surprising places — like the nonchalant acceptance by her son — but equally, there'd been prejudice and even hate mail.

Hate mail: she'd even received a couple of letters hand-delivered to the Brisbane hotel. "Why did you save that bitch Strickland?" the politest one had demanded, "Is she a butch dyke like you?"

As a detective assigned to difficult cases of high public interest, she had been accustomed to personal attacks, almost always anonymous. But the abuse had been about her competency, or suggestions that she had been paid off or influenced to come up with a particular finding in a case. To be attacked for her sexuality alone was new and disturbing.

Sitting on the Concert Hall stage with the other invited guests, Carol covertly checked her watch. Marla always kept her audience waiting a few minutes, and the anticipatory hum from the audience was growing louder. The Concert Hall held over two and a half thousand seats, the majority of them in a steeply angled block that looked down on the wide stage that more often than not held the Sydney Symphony Orchestra. The remainder of the seats were in a series of angled boxes that ran up both sides of the hall, each one higher than the one before. The blond wood of the walls and ceiling combined to form a gigantic arching lid from which a series of bizarre acoustic donuts hung suspended.

There were so many entrances from the terraced steps ascending between the inner and outer shells of the hall that additional officers had been deployed.

Even so, during Marla's entry Carol's skin prickled as she looked up at the ranks of applauding people.

The speaking desk was lined with kevlar; she'd insisted that Marla wear a heavier bullet-proof vest; officers were planted throughout the audience. In a venue like this, there was little more that she could do, other than put Marla behind bullet-proof glass — a suggestion that had been greeted with predictable scorn. "Carol, I'm not a feminist goldfish, for God's sake!"

Carol looked around at the other guests on the platform: high-profile women in business; feminist activists; politicians, including the ubiquitous Joseph Marin. She wondered if *he* wore a kevlar vest under his impeccably cut gray suit. Presumably he would claim, if challenged, that he was courting the women's vote for the next election, although his constituency contained many conservative women who might be offended by radical feminism.

Their eyes met. He smiled and nodded.

When the guests had been waiting to go onto the stage she'd been tempted to approach Marin and say, "Why did you use Richard Novell to pull strings to have me appointed as Marla Strickland's bodyguard?" but she was sure he'd raise his eyebrows and eschew any knowledge of the matter. And Bourke had said it was only a rumor, after all . . .

Now Marla was speaking, and the air vibrated around her as she spoke, her voice filling the huge hall with compelling intensity. Even Carol, her attention concentrated on any potential threat, felt her heart rise as Marla exulted, "Women can do anything! Anything! If we are together there is nothing we cannot achieve!"

163

The evening was a triumph. Afterwards, Marla was on a total high, bubbling with laughter at her achievement. There were bottles of French champagne in the dressing room, and Carol suddenly felt a need to speak with, to see, to touch, Madeline.

"Carol! Can't you have one glass of champagne?"

Deliberately sounding officious, Carol responded, "Please. Not while I'm on duty."

Bev Diaz gave a rare smile. "Can't you be bribed?"

"Most people have a price," said Pam Boyle sourly. She was ostentatiously holding a tumbler of water, and she took a sip before she added, "What's yours, Carol?"

"Whatever it is, no one's offered it yet."

Her levity didn't deflect Pam, whose expression was serious. "Would you do anything to save your own life?"

Carol, who was sweating under the weight of the kevlar vest she wore under her jacket, said lightly, "I certainly would."

Pam's mouth twisted. "Isn't your *duty*," she said unpleasantly, "to die if it means saving Marla?"

"That's not what it says in the manual —"

Carol broke off as Sid took her arm. "Can I see you outside?" Since her caustic words to him, he'd been playing it very cool, as though nothing had happened.

Anne was waiting in the corridor. "Carol, there's been an incident at the hotel . . ."

"A bomb?"

Sid grinned. "Nothing so dramatic. A bunch of skinheads roughed up the staff and laid waste to the lobby. There've been a couple of arrests, but I think

Marla had better cool her heels here for another half an hour or so."

"Was it random, or were they targeting her?"

"Not random," said Sid, "when you consider they spray-painted some *very* rude phrases about women in general and Ms. Strickland in particular."

The Family First protesters had long since departed, and, apart from a few couples strolling along the boardwalk to admire the arch of the Harbour Bridge and the huge tiled sails of the Opera House soaring above them, the forecourt was virtually deserted when the limousine drove out from the shelter of the passageway. Carol and Marla followed in the escort car. As they drew up behind the limo at the exit booth, their driver glanced back over his shoulder. "Successful evening, ladies?"

Before either could answer, he gave a grunt and slumped against the Huntling Security guard. Carol didn't need to hear the flat crack, see the spray of blood or the hole in the windscreen. "Get down!"

"Jesus!" said the guard beside the driver. "Oh, Jesus!" Another crack split the air, and he was silent.

Carol had shoved Marla onto the floor and lay over her. A handgun was useless in this situation, but the cold weight of it in her hand was some comfort. She could hear her own breath sobbing in her throat. The car was better protection than nothing, although high velocity bullets could go straight through the metal panels and explode in soft human flesh. Such deadly projectiles would only be stopped by the bulkiest of vests — kevlar with ceramic plates — but they were both wearing the lighter version. And nothing could protect their heads. Carol shut her eyes, reliving the memory of the paralyzing pain of the gunshot wound she'd received.

"Carol! Are you all right?"

Denise wrenched open the door. She was panting.

"It's okay. They've gone."

Carol got up slowly and helped Marla out of the car, deliberately shielding her from the front seat. Someone had opened the driver's door and was leaning in. A siren wailed in the distance. "Are they dead?"

The man, grim-faced, nodded. "Yes. Both head shots."

Marla stumbled as Carol pushed her gently towards Anne. "Take her back to the hotel and call a doctor."

Marla looked back at her, eyes enormous in a white face. Blood from the driver's head had sprayed across her cheek. "I don't need a doctor."

Carol patted her shoulder gently. "Please, Marla, don't argue. Not now." She watched the limousine drive away, then turned back to Denise. "Where was he?"

Denise gave her the ghost of a grin. "Funny how we never think a woman would be a sniper." She pointed to sandstone steps that led up the low cliff to the iron railings marking the boundary of the Botanic Gardens. "There was a Fed up there, just in case. The sniper, or someone with him, strangled her."

Carol's breath was easing and her heart resuming a metronomic beat. It was a familiar feeling: cold rage was arming her for battle. "Those skinheads at the hotel were timed to keep us here long enough to thin out the traffic and make targeting easier." She glanced back at the two bodies in the front seat. "Whoever was firing was good enough to get two head shots, so why isn't Marla dead? The telescopic night sight would have given a clear view and even a burst of automatic fire through the car would probably have got her."

"No time? We had people out of the limo and running, straight after the first shot."

Carol shook her head. "I think they still want Marla alive — for the moment."

CHAPTER FIFTEEN

The moment she had got back to the hotel, Carol called Aunt Sarah. "... Yes, I thought it would make the late newscasts. Look, Aunt Sarah, I can't talk now. I'm sure Justin will ring from Bali — they'll get the news there, too. Will you speak to David for me? Tell him I'm fine and I'll call him as soon as I can."

Carol broke the connection and punched in Madeline's number. "Madeline, it's me —"

"You're okay?"

"I'm fine. We're having a council of war here, so I'll call you in the morning."

"I don't care how late it is, Carol. When you can get back to me, please do."

No sooner had Carol replaced the receiver, than the phone rang again. She exclaimed impatiently, and Bev said, "It's all right, Carol, I'll take it in the other room and I'll monitor any other calls if you like."

Carol nodded wearily. "Thanks. That would be great."

Even tranquilized, Marla wouldn't rest. She joined everyone in the main room of the penthouse, her dark hair disheveled, her satin dressing gown pulled tight around her as though she were freezing. "He was talking to us, and then he was dead . . ." Her eyes focused on Keil Huntling, who'd come to the hotel as soon as he'd been told of the shooting. "I'm so sorry about what happened. It was *me* they were trying to kill."

Pam Boyle put an awkward arm around her shoulders. "Come back and lie down. The doctor said —"

"I don't care what the doctor said!" She flung Pam's arm away. "Just get me a drink, will you?"

When Pam looked irresolute, Carol said, "I'll get it. Sit down, Marla." She brought over Marla's vodka and tonic and a whiskey on the rocks for herself. Marla's hands were shaking, so Carol put the glass down on the table. "We're all having a drink tonight," she said with a gesture towards Sid's beer and Denise's vodka and orange, "I hope you don't mind."

Marla shook her head numbly. "I don't mind."

Keil Huntling had refused alcohol, and was sitting forward with his hands clasped between his knees.

169

"Inspector Ashton wants to terminate Huntling Security's involvement," he said to Marla, "but I want to remind you we have a contract."

"I can't think about that now. See Bev..."

"Where's your sister, Mr. Huntling?"

Carol's question wasn't welcome. Keil Huntling played with the knot of his tie as though it was too tight. "She's not available, and I can't see the point —"

"The point is that Cynthia Huntling set up all the security arrangements for the tour, then disappeared."

He sat back with a rough laugh. "God! I suppose you've got some far-fetched conspiracy theory, Inspector."

"Four people are dead, Mr. Huntling. One was your employee."

He sobered immediately. "Cynthia's not available. She's in the States." When Carol continued to look at him, he blustered, "I can't see why my sister's whereabouts can possibly be relevant."

"My information is that she's in a religious retreat in Colorado. Is that true?"

"Yes, but —"

"And who runs the retreat, Mr. Huntling?"

"A church."

Carol was inexorable. "It's the Church of God's Desire, isn't it? The one headed by Dr. Lucas Britt."

"Yes, but —"

"Please accompany Constable Anne Newsome to the other room. She has some questions and you'll be asked to make a formal statement tomorrow." When he seemed likely to refuse, she added, "This is a murder investigation, Mr. Huntling."

Marla watched him go with a look of disbelief.

"Huntling Security has something to do with Lucas Britt?"

"So it seems," said Sid. "We got a tip from one of Carol's men and followed it up in the United States."

Marla swiveled to look at Pam Boyle, who had joined Gary on the other side of the room. "*You* dealt with Cynthia Huntling, Pam."

"You told me to, Marla," she said firmly. "You said she was the only woman heading a security firm in Australia that could provide the services you wanted."

The flash of energy dissipated, Marla sank back into her chair. "Yes, I think I remember . . ."

"We'll talk tomorrow," said Carol, "but we've just been discussing the rest of your tour. The consensus is that you should cancel completely. There's absolutely no point in putting your life in further danger."

Marla let out her breath in a long sigh. "I agree about the public appearances, but I'll do the debate, and any other television."

Sprawled in a lounge chair, Gary stirred himself enough to say, "We should go back to the States tomorrow."

After a long steadying swallow of vodka, Marla said flatly, "I'm staying, but you can go, if you want to."

"It's not me they're after." There was a note of satisfaction in his voice. Carol thought what an unpleasant little tick he was, but she couldn't be bothered saying anything to him.

Marla finished her drink and sat looking at the empty glass in her hand. "You didn't catch anyone?"

"No." Sid was subdued. "The whole area's

cordoned off, but I'm sure whoever it was has got clean away." He stretched and yawned. "I think we should call it a night. There's nothing more we can do at the moment." He leaned over to pat Marla's knee. "And don't worry about security — I've got more agents in this hotel than there are guests."

Denise had been uncharacteristically silent and she only nodded wearily when Carol said, "Can I see you before you go?" Carol waited until they were alone, then said, "I want to know if there's any possible connection between either Joseph Marin or Richard Novell and Dr. Lucas Britt."

Her surprise obvious, Denise said, "If there is, it hasn't come up in any ASIO security clearance."

Carol smiled grimly. "It wouldn't, would it? I want full telephone records for Keil and Cynthia Huntling's private phones, as well as for their company. The same for Joseph Marin, Richard Novell and Lucas Britt. I'm interested in the last two years, especially regarding international calls to and from the States."

Denise pursed her lips. "Jeez, Carol, I'll have to kick this up the hierarchy . . . Marin's a pretty big fish to fry and all hell will break lose if he finds out —"

"Do it."

"Okay." Denise grinned. "I'd love to nail our Minister for Culture for something other than poor taste. So far he's been Teflon coated."

"One other thing —"

"Only one?" Denise mocked.

"Mark Bourke is getting names associated with the Paddington women's clinic bombing last year. I want the list checked against all those telephone records."

"Is *that* all?"

"I want it as soon as possible."

"Of course you do," said Denise.

Madeline didn't sound sleepy in the least. "Carol, thank you for calling back. I've been watching the late news — those shots must have been close to you."

Carol was warmed by her concern, but said laconically, "Close enough."

"I suppose it's an impossible dream to think I might see you tonight."

"Totally impossible. As it is now, I'll be with Marla until she leaves the country."

"So I have only my memories . . ." Madeline sighed theatrically.

Although she felt too exhausted for any in-depth conversation, Carol heard herself saying, "Madeline, how serious is this for you?"

A heartbeat, then, "Serious."

"Have you considered your career? I'm out of the closet, whether I chose it or not. You aren't."

"Come on, Carol," she protested, "this is a bit heavy for right now, isn't it?"

"It's something we need to discuss, but you're right, now is hardly the time."

After she'd hung up, Madeline's last words lingered: "Darling, if it's important, we can work it out."

CHAPTER SIXTEEN

Carol was wearing dark pants and a long-sleeved rose shirt that concealed her holstered gun. The heat of the lights made her grateful that neither she nor Marla were wearing kevlar vests in the studio.

Madeline came over. "I've told Charlie, my floor manager, to let you stand wherever you like. He'll tell you if you're in the way of a camera."

Resolutely pushing away the vision she had of Madeline lying in her arms, Carol clicked into the cool working persona with which she was most comfortable. "It concerns me that this a live broadcast, Madeline. That means Wellspring knows where and when."

That Joseph Marin knows where and when. It had taken Denise a few days of concentrated effort, but ASIO had done a preliminary analysis of the telephone records Carol had requested and the telltale calls had been there. Nothing was to be done to alert any potential Wellspring members, but the key names were under twenty-four hour surveillance. But of course, there were the unidentified Wellspring agents out in the field . . .

The floodlights burnished Madeline's hair and accentuated the strong line of her jaw. She wore a teal blue dress that deepened the dark gray of her eyes. "Where and when is all very well, but I'd be more worried about *how,* if I were Wellspring. The whole studio's as tight as a drum — not only has it been searched twice for bombs, each person has been through a metal detector *and* a personal search and had every bag or purse emptied. Unless someone leaps up and tries to strangle Marla in front of us, I can't see how she can be attacked." She grinned mischievously. "Would you like the water glasses replaced with paper cups on the off-chance that Dr. Britt smashes one and slashes her?"

Carol said stubbornly, "I don't feel good about this interview."

"Carol, I'm not going to call it off. And it's not only that the ratings are going to be phenomenal, it's also going to be exciting television, and I want *my* show to be the one that gets it to air."

"If there's any danger, you'll be in the middle of it."

"If I didn't know better, I'd think you cared."

Carol didn't smile at Madeline's mockery. "I do care, very much."

Madeline touched Carol's hand lightly. "I won't be in any danger."

"Madeline, listen." Carol spoke urgently to convince her. "Wellspring didn't want to kill Marla before. There wouldn't have been enough publicity. But the apparent attempts on her life, the death of those three people . . . Everything's been orchestrated to make whatever happens to Marla Strickland from now on a media sensation. This program tonight has already been picked up by the networks in the States, hasn't it?"

She nodded slowly. "Apart from America, we've sold internationally, particularly in Europe."

Rubbing her forehead as though she could remove the conviction that she'd overlooked something, Carol said, "Can't you see that this gives Wellspring a perfect stage for an execution? Lucas Britt condemns her to the world, then someone kills her."

"On live television? Who? Lucas Britt himself? Someone in Marla Strickland's staff? My crew? Everyone working in the studio has been checked out, and anyway my staff has been with me for years. I'd trust every last one of them."

Carol felt the suffocating force of certainty. "I don't know *who,* except it won't be Lucas Britt personally — he'd use someone else. And I don't know *how.* There aren't any weapons here. I've had anything potentially lethal removed." She smiled faintly. "I've been paranoid enough to worry about the drinks or food being poisoned, or the air-conditioning used to feed something deadly into the studio."

"Darling Carol," Madeline said softly. "When this is over . . ."

"You don't know how much I want Marla Strickland and her staff safely on a plane and winging their way across the Pacific."

Madeline's grin had a wicked edge. "Not half as much as I do. I'd love to know what you're like when I have your full attention."

Carol used her most reasonable tone. "I want to put your staff in the control room. You'll be able to see them, and speak with them, but they won't be here in the studio."

Marla was clearly nervous, moving from foot to foot as she clasped her leather folder close to her chest like a talisman. "I don't want any changes, Carol. During the commercial breaks I want to be able to speak with Bev in particular, but I could have questions that only Pam could answer on direct mailing and advertising . . ." She made a petulant gesture. "Look, this is important and I want everything as it always is, okay?"

"You don't need Gary."

"Jesus!" Marla exploded, "just leave it, Carol!"

Carol stood as close as she could to *The Shipley Report* set, which was composed of a huge semi-circular cream-colored desk supported on contoured columns. Madeline was seated in the middle with Lucas Britt to her left and Marla to her right. Off set, Lucas Britt's assistant, a substantial middle-aged man in a tight-fitting blue suit, sat with folded arms on a metal chair out of the way against the wall. Both Pam Boyle and Bev Diaz stood near him, but Gary had commandeered a battered armchair near the back of the studio.

Flexing her shoulders to release some of the tightness, Carol double-checked positions: Anne on the other side of the set close to Lucas Britt; Denise in the control room; Sid and one of his men at the studio door.

The monitor was showing the end of the news, with the aging male personality doing his trademark paper shuffle as he signed off. This was followed by a breathless promo for the debate and the advertisements for the car company sponsoring it.

Obeying the director's voice in their headphones, the camera operators glided their hulking cameras in an elaborate ritual, one moving forward as the other retreated. The floor manager, earphones in place, was stepping confidently over the obstacles presented by the cables that snaked everywhere over the floor.

He gestured to Madeline, "Ten seconds," then began the silent countdown for her with his fingers. On cue she smiled, and Carol could imagine the countless screens where her palpable charm flowed out to warm her audience. Her introduction outlined the careers of her guests with brevity and then she set the conditions of the debate: each person would make a short introductory statement, then Madeline would moderate as they discussed the issues raised. When they had first arrived in the studio they'd drawn lots to see who would speak first, and Britt had won. "God's will," he'd remarked.

In the full glare of the studio lights Lucas Britt's white hair formed a radiant halo to frame his kindly face. His color was high, his smile serene.

He began gently, "It is God's intention that every person play his or her part in the pattern the Almighty has designed for our happiness." His voice took on a sterner timbre. "So why the suffering of God's people? Why is there dreadful crime after dreadful crime? We hear every day of the breakdown of society, of the appalling abuse of the young, of the virtual desertion of the old by their children . . ." A pause, then he flung out his arm to point dramatically at Marla. "It is because of this woman! *And* others like her. In their arrogance, they believe God's way can be abandoned. It cannot!" He dropped his hand and shook his head sorrowfully. "These women disturb God's natural order, and chaos results."

Marla had listened to him impassively, her chin high. Carol could see no trace of nervousness on her face, although her fingers played with the edge of her document folder. When the camera's red light glowed, indicating she was now on the screen, her lips curved in her usual assured smile. "I will be speaking to you about self-respect. Something that every individual should have as a birthright. But self-respect can be fleeting when you have been disregarded, have been violated, have seen opportunities others have snatched away. And in our culture this happens to millions, simply because they are women." She let a moment pass. "What is the rationale behind this? The justification for the denigration of half the population of the world? Ask the male-dominated religions." Another interval to emphasize the last point, then

179

she continued, "In our society *every* woman, at some time, has been denied self-respect, has felt that she is less important, less esteemed, less able. That is the lie that has to be destroyed."

Marla gestured with an open hand toward Lucas Britt. "The so-called natural order that Dr. Britt says we must follow is not natural at all. It is based on gender slavery cleverly disguised as religion. Make no mistake: independence, education, freedom — these are reserved for males in Dr. Britt's ideal world. Tell this to your sisters, tell this to your daughters: unless we stand together, unless we fight the forces who want to keep us weak, all our lives we will have less power, less money, less freedom . . ."

When Marla finished her introductory remarks, Madeline smoothly came in with a question to Lucas Britt. She let him answer fully, but expertly cut him off before he could use the question as a springboard to something further. Then it was Marla's turn to speak.

The floor manager signaled a commercial break. When the ads started to roll on the monitor, the professional tension in the crew immediately lessened. Madeline stood to brush the creases out of her skirt, Lucas Britt took a sip of water. Gary heaved himself out of his chair and came forward to examine the set. Marla turned her head as Bev called out, "You missed an important point in that last response. The figures are in your folder."

Marla flicked over the pages. "Where? Come and show me."

Bev raised her eyebrows as Carol stepped onto the

set with her. "Don't you trust me, Carol? Think I'm going to karate chop Marla on national television?" She turned her back on Carol and took the folder from Marla. "Look, here's where I mean — the disparity of research funds devoted to women's health. You need to emphasize how all the research on heart trouble is based on *men*, not women . . ."

The floor manager said, "Ten seconds." The relaxed crew was suddenly alert.

Bev handed back the folder. "Marla, I'll stay close by to help you in the next commercial break." She stepped off the set to stand just outside the bright circle of light.

When the program restarted, Lucas Britt launched into a spirited attack on Marla Strickland's supporters: ". . . they are deviates, men-hating lesbians, childless women whose shrunken souls can only envy mothers and wives who are content within the protection of their husbands' authority —"

A movement caught Carol's eye. Pam Boyle was carefully making her way over the floor obstructions to join Bev Diaz. She watched them exchange a few words, her mind slipping back to a conversation she'd had before the program began. What had Madeline said? ". . . each person has been through a metal detector and a personal search, and had every bag or purse emptied . . ."

But that wasn't true. Marla Strickland was the potential victim, so she hadn't been through a detector and she hadn't been searched. And all she'd brought with her to the studio was a black leather folder . . .

Marla was replying to Lucas Britt's attack, speaking into the camera as though to a real person, her voice ringing with passionate persuasion.

Carol looked at the folder lying open on the cream-colored surface of the desk.

Marla had carried the weapon that was to kill her into the studio.

Carol and Bev Diaz moved at almost the same moment, but Carol was too far away.

Startled, Marla looked up as Bev loomed behind her. The thin blade flashed in the brilliant lighting as she stabbed down at Marla's exposed throat.

Carol had no time to get close enough to disarm her. From the other side of the wide desk she swept her right arm in a parody of a tennis backhand, desperately attempting to interrupt the slender weapon's deadly arc.

The blade stung like fire as it slashed through the thin cotton of Carol's shirt and into her forearm. It wasn't enough to deflect the blade completely. As though in slow motion, Carol saw blood spurt from Marla's shoulder.

Marla twisted in her chair, screaming as she held up her hands in vain protection. Bev brought her arm up for the next blow.

Carol flung herself across the desk. Disregarding the dagger, she seized the collar of Bev's polo shirt. With her full weight and all the strength in her shoulders, she yanked the woman towards her. Bev stabbed at her eyes.

She jerked her head away. The sting of the blade slicing her cheek filled Carol with red rage. She had Bev spread-eagled across the desk: Marla was out of immediate danger. Bev struggled wildly, slashing with the bloodied weapon. Carol released the shirt collar to seize her wrist with one hand while she chopped hard at her windpipe with the edge of the other.

Bev gave an inarticulate sound. The blade dropped from her hand and spun across the surface of the table. Exultant, Carol drew back her hand to strike again. Bev looked up at her, open-mouthed, gagging.

"We've got her, Carol!"

She let her arm drop, suddenly aware of the blood soaking her sleeve. She stood stupidly as Anne and Sid wrestled Bev face down off the desk. Blood was running in a steady stream through her fingers and onto the floor.

"Oh, darling..." Madeline had an arm around her. "You're bleeding —" She gave a half-hysterical laugh, "— all over my set."

CHAPTER SEVENTEEN

Carol looked around the light-filled penthouse suite. She didn't want to be in this debriefing session for Marla. She wanted to be outside in the sun and wind, to be with her son and his innocence, to ignore mean thoughts and petty jealousies, to escape from the knowledge that irrational hatred could transform ordinary people into avenging killers who were persuaded that they were beyond the law because they were carrying out the will of an unmerciful God.

Her glance circled the table: Anne Newsome, sitting alert and silent; Pam Boyle, folded awkwardly into her chair; Sid Safer, lounging nonchalantly, coat and knees open; Gary, fingers tapping an impatient tattoo; Denise relaxed and cheerful. Nearby Marla, her arm in a sling, reclined on a sofa positioned so she could look out at the activity on the harbor.

"So," said Denise, "we've established that Wellspring had ambitions to become an international conspiracy, taking its foot soldiers from fundamentalist religious organizations involved in what they see as a righteous fight against abortion, gay rights and feminism. Wellspring's leaders had rather wider political ambitions — the pursuit of power. And the rising tide of fundamentalism encouraged them to make conservatives their constituency." She gestured towards Carol. "I'm embarrassed to admit that both the Feds and ASIO failed to finger Joseph Marin, the leader of the Australian faction. His network included like-minded individuals such as Cynthia and Keil Huntling and extended to the most extreme right-wing groups, though the majority of them had no idea how violent Wellspring could really be."

"So you were right, Carol." Sid Safer's voice held no pleasure. "You got lucky."

There was malice in Denise's smile. "Nose out of joint, Sid? Surprised someone in the State police force could out-think you? Or is it the fact that it's a woman?"

Marla turned her head to say, "Perhaps Sid's upset because Carol's a gay woman, as well."

"That's bullshit!"

Marla swung her feet to the floor. "I've overheard you say a few things, Sid, especially to Gary. 'Dyke' was probably the nicest word you used."

Sid looked at her stonily. "It's a free world,

Marla. I can say what like." He sat back, arms folded.

"You're a dinosaur, Sid," said Denise pleasantly, "and you can't become extinct too soon."

Marla, her face white and pinched, slid carefully onto an empty chair between Anne and Pam. "I want to know about Bev. I would have trusted her with my life."

At a glance from Carol, Anne shuffled her notes and said formally, "Beverly Diaz had a family history of alcoholism and she was terrified she was going to repeat the self-destructive pattern she'd seen in her mother. She attended AA meetings and joined a support group for the families of substance abusers. Then she heard of drug and alcohol clinics run by the Church of God's Desire and admitted herself to a residential program in one, becoming very involved in the workings of the church itself. Being intelligent, but emotionally vulnerable and obsessive, she was excellent material for indoctrination. She's given us full details of how she was recruited, trained and sent undercover to infiltrate Strickland Enterprises. Because she had a genuine history of success in management positions, she had no trouble being hired." Anne looked up at Marla. "For what it's worth, she said she grew quite fond of you and had some regret that she had to kill you."

"A comfort." Marla attempted a smile.

"It was all planned well ahead," said Carol. "Bev subtly pushed Huntling Security as a company to be supported because it was owned by a woman, although she made sure it was Pam Boyle who negotiated a contract. In Australia she played out a scene with Keil Huntling for my benefit, where she challenged him about costs. Having Huntling Security involved wasn't essential to Wellspring, but was desirable because it meant that Marla's movements would always be known, including which car she'd be traveling in as she went to and from engagements. A ring-in Huntling guard planted the mock bomb at Sydney University while apparently doing a security check. Apart from that, being involved in security arrangements gave unrestricted access to Marla, although it had been decided that her execution was to be a very public affair."

Gary stretched his interlocked fingers until they cracked. "Bev couldn't have thought there was any way she'd escape from the TV studio. She was stupid to try to get Marla there."

Pam stared at him from across the table, her dislike clear. "It should be obvious, even to you, Gary, that Bev wanted to kill Marla on national television because she believed it would be seen as a judgment and then a public execution. She let the program run long enough for Lucas Britt to condemn her, then Bev tried to carry out the sentence."

He snorted scornfully. "She had to be off her head. Who wants to get caught red-handed like that?"

"Bev did. Because she knew the media would go wild over her trial, which could then be used as a platform to broadcast Wellspring's beliefs. Bev saw herself as a martyr, Gary. Something *you'd* never understand."

Carol looked at Pam thoughtfully. *You have the stuff of martyrs in you — that combination of personal arrogance and total subservience to a set of beliefs.*

Marla fingered her throat. "Carol, that dagger. I dream about it . . ."

"Your leather folder was made with a hollow spine so that the blade would fit into it," said Carol. "I didn't think much of it at the time, but you'd mentioned that the folder was a gift from your staff. There was no reason for you to know that Bev had not only suggested the gift, but helpfully supplied it."

Marla looked stricken. "She knew how she would kill me, that far ahead? But she worked for me . . . We were friends . . ."

There was little comfort Carol could give, but she said, "Try and see Bev as a skilled actor, playing a part to achieve something she totally believed in. She was very convincing, even confronting me with demands that Madeline Shipley favor you during the debate with Lucas Britt. And she was deliberately secretive about her attendance at AA meetings, knowing we would check back and find she had a genuine reason to be there. It was all part of the role she was playing for Wellspring."

"Bev seemed to *believe* all the things I stand for." Marla bit her lip. "How could she have fooled me so well?"

"And me." Pam Boyle's voice was as bitter as her face. "The bitch fooled me, too."

Carol knew they both felt betrayed at a deeply personal level. She said to Marla, "Remember what Anne told you. Bev liked you as a person — the Marla Strickland she tried to kill was the outspoken feminist the public knew."

"But with a knife —"

"Bev knew from past experience that you, as the potential target, would not be searched. The weapon had to be something that could be completely concealed, yet easy to get at when needed."

Carol's tone was businesslike. "The blade is thin tempered steel, and razor-sharp. It fits the hollow spine of your folder exactly and during the commercial break she slipped it out to conceal in her clothes while she was showing you information she said you needed."

Marla shook her head. "I know you're telling me the truth, Carol, but I can't believe it."

"It was planned to the last detail," said Carol grimly. "There was no room in the spine of the folder to fit a dagger with a handle, so Bev wound layers of cloth tape around the blunt end of the blade to have a non-slip grip."

"She *is* insane, isn't she?"

"Not legally. No."

Sid sat forward to put his elbows on his spread knees. "Why don't you tell Marla why you were chosen as her bodyguard?" His tone was unpleasant. "You've forgotten to mention *that*."

"Because Carol's a lesbian," said Pam. She said the last word as though it had a nasty taste.

"Lesbian," Denise repeated, "is a fascinating word that always gets a strong response. The radical right uses gay or lesbian as shorthand terms for abominable and unnatural — and excitingly sinful — behavior. And having Marla with a high profile bodyguard who was open about her sexuality equaled guilt by association — Marla was proud to call herself a feminist — maybe she was worse! Maybe she was queer, too."

Carol looked at Sid's implacable face. He was jealous of her success and threatened by her sexual identity. She was abruptly conscious of her physical self. Her side ached, the slash across her cheek burned under the dressing, her arm throbbed.

Suddenly she wanted to be somewhere else — anywhere else. She needed Aunt Sarah's acceptance... the love of her son...

The phone on the bar rang. Pam went to answer it. "It's for you." She held out the receiver to Carol.

Let it be Madeline.

It was.

A few of the publications of
THE NAIAD PRESS, INC.
P.O. Box 10543 • Tallahassee, Florida 32302
Phone (904) 539-5965
Toll-Free Order Number: 1-800-533-1973
Mail orders welcome. Please include 15% postage.

OPEN HOUSE by Pat Welch. 176 pp. P.I. Helen Black's fourth
case. ISBN 1-56280-102-3 $10.95

ONCE MORE WITH FEELING by Peggy J. Herring. 240 pp.
Lighthearted, loving romantic adventure. ISBN 1-56280-089-2 10.95

FOREVER by Evelyn Kennedy. 224 pp. Passionate romance — love
overcoming all obstacles. ISBN 1-56280-094-9 10.95

WHISPERS by Kris Bruyer. 176 pp. Romantic ghost story
ISBN 1-56280-082-5 10.95

NIGHT SONGS by Penny Mickelbury. 224 pp. A Gianna
Maglione Mystery. Second in a series. ISBN 1-56280-097-3 10.95

GETTING TO THE POINT by Teresa Stores. 256 pp. Classic
southern Lesbian novel. ISBN 1-56280-100-7 10.95

PAINTED MOON by Karin Kallmaker. 224 pp. Delicious
Kallmaker romance. ISBN 1-56280-075-2 9.95

THE MYSTERIOUS NAIAD edited by Katherine V. Forrest &
Barbara Grier. 320 pp. Love stories by Naiad Press authors.
ISBN 1-56280-074-4 14.95

DAUGHTERS OF A CORAL DAWN by Katherine V. Forrest.
240 pp. Tenth Anniversay Edition. ISBN 1-56280-104-X 10.95

BODY GUARD by Claire McNab. 208 pp. A Carol Ashton Mystery.
6th in a series. ISBN 1-56280-073-6 9.95

CACTUS LOVE by Lee Lynch. 192 pp. Stories by the beloved
storyteller. ISBN 1-56280-071-X 9.95

SECOND GUESS by Rose Beecham. 216 pp. An Amanda Valentine
Mystery. 2nd in a series. ISBN 1-56280-069-8 9.95

THE SURE THING by Melissa Hartman. 208 pp. L.A. earthquake
romance. ISBN 1-56280-078-7 9.95

A RAGE OF MAIDENS by Lauren Wright Douglas. 240 pp. A
Caitlin Reece Mystery. 6th in a series. ISBN 1-56280-068-X 9.95

TRIPLE EXPOSURE by Jackie Calhoun. 224 pp. Romantic drama
involving many characters. ISBN 1-56280-067-1 9.95

UP, UP AND AWAY by Catherine Ennis. 192 pp. Delightful
romance. ISBN 1-56280-065-5   9.95

PERSONAL ADS by Robbi Sommers. 176 pp. Sizzling short
stories. ISBN 1-56280-059-0   9.95

FLASHPOINT by Katherine V. Forrest. 256 pp. Lesbian
blockbuster! ISBN 1-56280-043-4   22.95

CROSSWORDS by Penny Sumner. 256 pp. 2nd Victoria Cross
Mystery. ISBN 1-56280-064-7   9.95

SWEET CHERRY WINE by Carol Schmidt. 224 pp. A novel of
suspense. ISBN 1-56280-063-9   9.95

CERTAIN SMILES by Dorothy Tell. 160 pp. Erotic short stories.
ISBN 1-56280-066-3   9.95

EDITED OUT by Lisa Haddock. 224 pp. 1st Carmen Ramirez
Mystery. ISBN 1-56280-077-9   9.95

WEDNESDAY NIGHTS by Camarin Grae. 288 pp. Sexy
adventure. ISBN 1-56280-060-4   10.95

SMOKEY O by Celia Cohen. 176 pp. Relationships on the
playing field. ISBN 1-56280-057-4   9.95

KATHLEEN O'DONALD by Penny Hayes. 256 pp. Rose and
Kathleen find each other and employment in 1909 NYC.
ISBN 1-56280-070-1   9.95

STAYING HOME by Elisabeth Nonas. 256 pp. Molly and Alix
want a baby . . . or do they? ISBN 1-56280-076-0   10.95

TRUE LOVE by Jennifer Fulton. 240 pp. Six lesbians searching
for love in all the "right" places. ISBN 1-56280-035-3   9.95

GARDENIAS WHERE THERE ARE NONE by Molleen Zanger.
176 pp. Why is Melanie inextricably drawn to the old house?
ISBN 1-56280-056-6   9.95

KEEPING SECRETS by Penny Mickelbury. 208 pp. A Gianna
Maglione Mystery. First in a series. ISBN 1-56280-052-3   9.95

THE ROMANTIC NAIAD edited by Katherine V. Forrest &
Barbara Grier. 336 pp. Love stories by Naiad Press authors.
ISBN 1-56280-054-X   14.95

UNDER MY SKIN by Jaye Maiman. 336 pp. A Robin Miller
mystery. 3rd in a series. ISBN 1-56280-049-3.   10.95

STAY TOONED by Rhonda Dicksion. 144 pp. Cartoons — 1st
collection since *Lesbian Survival Manual.* ISBN 1-56280-045-0   9.95

CAR POOL by Karin Kallmaker. 272pp. Lesbians on wheels
and then some! ISBN 1-56280-048-5   9.95

NOT TELLING MOTHER: STORIES FROM A LIFE by Diane
Salvatore. 176 pp. Her 3rd novel. ISBN 1-56280-044-2   9.95

GOBLIN MARKET by Lauren Wright Douglas. 240pp. A Caitlin
Reece Mystery. 5th in a series.   ISBN 1-56280-047-7   10.95

LONG GOODBYES by Nikki Baker. 256 pp. A Virginia Kelly
mystery. 3rd in a series.   ISBN 1-56280-042-6   9.95

FRIENDS AND LOVERS by Jackie Calhoun. 224 pp. Mid-western
Lesbian lives and loves.   ISBN 1-56280-041-8   10.95

THE CAT CAME BACK by Hilary Mullins. 208 pp. Highly
praised Lesbian novel.   ISBN 1-56280-040-X   9.95

BEHIND CLOSED DOORS by Robbi Sommers. 192 pp. Hot,
erotic short stories.   ISBN 1-56280-039-6   9.95

CLAIRE OF THE MOON by Nicole Conn. 192 pp. See the
movie — read the book!   ISBN 1-56280-038-8   10.95

SILENT HEART by Claire McNab. 192 pp. Exotic Lesbian
romance.   ISBN 1-56280-036-1   10.95

HAPPY ENDINGS by Kate Brandt. 272 pp. Intimate conversations
with Lesbian authors.   ISBN 1-56280-050-7   10.95

THE SPY IN QUESTION by Amanda Kyle Williams. 256 pp.
4th Madison McGuire.   ISBN 1-56280-037-X   9.95

SAVING GRACE by Jennifer Fulton. 240 pp. Adventure and
romantic entanglement.   ISBN 1-56280-051-5   9.95

THE YEAR SEVEN by Molleen Zanger. 208 pp. Women surviving
in a new world.   ISBN 1-56280-034-5   9.95

CURIOUS WINE by Katherine V. Forrest. 176 pp. Tenth Anniver-
sary Edition. The most popular contemporary Lesbian love story.
                                          ISBN 1-56280-053-1   10.95
     Audio Book (2 cassettes)   ISBN 1-56280-105-8   16.95

CHAUTAUQUA by Catherine Ennis. 192 pp. Exciting, romantic
adventure.   ISBN 1-56280-032-9   9.95

A PROPER BURIAL by Pat Welch. 192 pp. A Helen Black
mystery. 3rd in a series.   ISBN 1-56280-033-7   9.95

SILVERLAKE HEAT: A Novel of Suspense by Carol Schmidt.
240 pp. Rhonda is as hot as Laney's dreams.   ISBN 1-56280-031-0   9.95

LOVE, ZENA BETH by Diane Salvatore. 224 pp. The most talked
about lesbian novel of the nineties!   ISBN 1-56280-030-2   10.95

A DOORYARD FULL OF FLOWERS by Isabel Miller. 160 pp.
Stories incl. 2 sequels to *Patience and Sarah.*   ISBN 1-56280-029-9   9.95

MURDER BY TRADITION by Katherine V. Forrest. 288 pp. A
Kate Delafield Mystery. 4th in a series. ISBN 1-56280-002-7   9.95

THE EROTIC NAIAD edited by Katherine V. Forrest & Barbara
Grier. 224 pp. Love stories by Naiad Press authors.
                                          ISBN 1-56280-026-4   13.95

DEAD CERTAIN by Claire McNab. 224 pp. A Carol Ashton
mystery. 5th in a series.   ISBN 1-56280-027-2   9.95

CRAZY FOR LOVING by Jaye Maiman. 320 pp. A Robin Miller
mystery. 2nd in a series.   ISBN 1-56280-025-6   9.95

STONEHURST by Barbara Johnson. 176 pp. Passionate regency
romance.   ISBN 1-56280-024-8   9.95

INTRODUCING AMANDA VALENTINE by Rose Beecham.
256 pp. An Amanda Valentine Mystery. First in a series.
                                             ISBN 1-56280-021-3   9.95

UNCERTAIN COMPANIONS by Robbi Sommers. 204 pp.
Steamy, erotic novel.   ISBN 1-56280-017-5   9.95

A TIGER'S HEART by Lauren W. Douglas. 240 pp. A Caitlin
Reece mystery. 4th in a series.   ISBN 1-56280-018-3   9.95

PAPERBACK ROMANCE by Karin Kallmaker. 256 pp. A
delicious romance.   ISBN 1-56280-019-1   9.95

MORTON RIVER VALLEY by Lee Lynch. 304 pp. Lee Lynch
at her best!   ISBN 1-56280-016-7   9.95

THE LAVENDER HOUSE MURDER by Nikki Baker. 224 pp.
A Virginia Kelly Mystery. 2nd in a series.   ISBN 1-56280-012-4   9.95

PASSION BAY by Jennifer Fulton. 224 pp. Passionate romance,
virgin beaches, tropical skies.   ISBN 1-56280-028-0   10.95

STICKS AND STONES by Jackie Calhoun. 208 pp. Contemporary
lesbian lives and loves.   ISBN 1-56280-020-5   9.95
Audio Book (2 cassettes)   ISBN 1-56280-106-6   16.95

DELIA IRONFOOT by Jeane Harris. 192 pp. Adventure for Delia
and Beth in the Utah mountains.   ISBN 1-56280-014-0   9.95

UNDER THE SOUTHERN CROSS by Claire McNab. 192 pp.
Romantic nights Down Under.   ISBN 1-56280-011-6   9.95

GRASSY FLATS by Penny Hayes. 256 pp. Lesbian romance in
the '30s.   ISBN 1-56280-010-8   9.95

A SINGULAR SPY by Amanda K. Williams. 192 pp. 3rd
Madison McGuire.   ISBN 1-56280-008-6   8.95

THE END OF APRIL by Penny Sumner. 240 pp. A Victoria
Cross mystery. First in a series.   ISBN 1-56280-007-8   8.95

HOUSTON TOWN by Deborah Powell. 208 pp. A Hollis
Carpenter mystery.   ISBN 1-56280-006-X   8.95

KISS AND TELL by Robbi Sommers. 192 pp. Scorching stories
by the author of *Pleasures*.   ISBN 1-56280-005-1   10.95

STILL WATERS by Pat Welch. 208 pp. A Helen Black mystery.
2nd in a series.   ISBN 0-941483-97-5   9.95

TO LOVE AGAIN by Evelyn Kennedy. 208 pp. Wildly romantic
love story.   ISBN 0-941483-85-1   9.95

IN THE GAME by Nikki Baker. 192 pp. A Virginia Kelly
mystery. First in a series. ISBN 1-56280-004-3 9.95

AVALON by Mary Jane Jones. 256 pp. A Lesbian Arthurian
romance. ISBN 0-941483-96-7 9.95

STRANDED by Camarin Grae. 320 pp. Entertaining, riveting
adventure. ISBN 0-941483-99-1 9.95

THE DAUGHTERS OF ARTEMIS by Lauren Wright Douglas.
240 pp. A Caitlin Reece mystery. 3rd in a series.
ISBN 0-941483-95-9 9.95

CLEARWATER by Catherine Ennis. 176 pp. Romantic secrets
of a small Louisiana town. ISBN 0-941483-65-7 8.95

THE HALLELUJAH MURDERS by Dorothy Tell. 176 pp. A
Poppy Dillworth mystery. 2nd in a series. ISBN 0-941483-88-6 8.95

SECOND CHANCE by Jackie Calhoun. 256 pp. Contemporary
Lesbian lives and loves. ISBN 0-941483-93-2 9.95

BENEDICTION by Diane Salvatore. 272 pp. Striking, contemporary romantic novel. ISBN 0-941483-90-8 9.95

BLACK IRIS by Jeane Harris. 192 pp. Caroline's hidden past . . .
ISBN 0-941483-68-1 8.95

TOUCHWOOD by Karin Kallmaker. 240 pp. Loving, May/
December romance. ISBN 0-941483-76-2 9.95

COP OUT by Claire McNab. 208 pp. A Carol Ashton mystery.
4th in a series. ISBN 0-941483-84-3 9.95

THE BEVERLY MALIBU by Katherine V. Forrest. 288 pp. A
Kate Delafield Mystery. 3rd in a series. ISBN 0-941483-48-7 10.95

THAT OLD STUDEBAKER by Lee Lynch. 272 pp. Andy's affair
with Regina and her attachment to her beloved car.
ISBN 0-941483-82-7 9.95

PASSION'S LEGACY by Lori Paige. 224 pp. Sarah is swept into
the arms of Augusta Pym in this delightful historical romance.
ISBN 0-941483-81-9 8.95

THE PROVIDENCE FILE by Amanda Kyle Williams. 256 pp.
Second Madison McGuire ISBN 0-941483-92-4 8.95

I LEFT MY HEART by Jaye Maiman. 320 pp. A Robin Miller
Mystery. First in a series. ISBN 0-941483-72-X 9.95

THE PRICE OF SALT by Patricia Highsmith (writing as Claire
Morgan). 288 pp. Classic lesbian novel, first issued in 1952 . . .
acknowledged by its author under her own, very famous, name.
ISBN 1-56280-003-5 9.95

SIDE BY SIDE by Isabel Miller. 256 pp. From beloved author of
Patience and Sarah. ISBN 0-941483-77-0 9.95

STAYING POWER: LONG TERM LESBIAN COUPLES by
Susan E. Johnson. 352 pp. Joys of coupledom. ISBN 0-941-483-75-4 14.95

IN EVERY PORT by Karin Kallmaker. 228 pp. Jessica's sexy,
adventuresome travels.   ISBN 0-941483-37-7   9.95

OF LOVE AND GLORY by Evelyn Kennedy. 192 pp. Exciting
WWII romance.   ISBN 0-941483-32-0   8.95

CLICKING STONES by Nancy Tyler Glenn. 288 pp. Love
transcending time.   ISBN 0-941483-31-2   9.95

SOUTH OF THE LINE by Catherine Ennis. 216 pp. Civil War
adventure.   ISBN 0-941483-29-0   8.95

WOMAN PLUS WOMAN by Dolores Klaich. 300 pp. Supurb
Lesbian overview.   ISBN 0-941483-28-2   9.95

THE FINER GRAIN by Denise Ohio. 216 pp. Brilliant young
college lesbian novel.   ISBN 0-941483-11-8   8.95

OCTOBER OBSESSION by Meredith More. Josie's rich, secret
Lesbian life.   ISBN 0-941483-18-5   8.95

BEFORE STONEWALL: THE MAKING OF A GAY AND
LESBIAN COMMUNITY by Andrea Weiss & Greta Schiller.
96 pp., 25 illus.   ISBN 0-941483-20-7   7.95

OSTEN'S BAY by Zenobia N. Vole. 204 pp. Sizzling adventure
romance set on Bonaire.   ISBN 0-941483-15-0   8.95

LESSONS IN MURDER by Claire McNab. 216 pp. A Carol
Ashton mystery. First in a series.   ISBN 0-941483-14-2   9.95

YELLOWTHROAT by Penny Hayes. 240 pp. Margarita, bandit,
kidnaps Julia.   ISBN 0-941483-10-X   8.95

SAPPHISTRY: THE BOOK OF LESBIAN SEXUALITY by
Pat Califia. 3d edition, revised. 208 pp. ISBN 0-941483-24-X   10.95

CHERISHED LOVE by Evelyn Kennedy. 192 pp. Erotic Lesbian
love story.   ISBN 0-941483-08-8   9.95

THE SECRET IN THE BIRD by Camarin Grae. 312 pp. Striking,
psychological suspense novel.   ISBN 0-941483-05-3   8.95

TO THE LIGHTNING by Catherine Ennis. 208 pp. Romantic
Lesbian 'Robinson Crusoe' adventure.   ISBN 0-941483-06-1   8.95

DREAMS AND SWORDS by Katherine V. Forrest. 192 pp.
Romantic, erotic, imaginative stories.   ISBN 0-941483-03-7   8.95

MEMORY BOARD by Jane Rule. 336 pp. Memorable novel
about an aging Lesbian couple.   ISBN 0-941483-02-9   10.95

THE ALWAYS ANONYMOUS BEAST by Lauren Wright Douglas.
224 pp. A Caitlin Reece mystery. First in a series.
                                          ISBN 0-941483-04-5   8.95

PARENTS MATTER by Ann Muller. 240 pp. Parents' relationships with Lesbian daughters and gay sons. ISBN 0-930044-91-6   9.95

THE BLACK AND WHITE OF IT by Ann Allen Shockley.
144 pp. Short stories.   ISBN 0-930044-96-7   7.95

SAY JESUS AND COME TO ME by Ann Allen Shockley. 288 pp. Contemporary romance. ISBN 0-930044-98-3   8.95

MURDER AT THE NIGHTWOOD BAR by Katherine V. Forrest. 240 pp. A Kate Delafield mystery. Second in a series. ISBN 0-930044-92-4   10.95

WINGED DANCER by Camarin Grae. 228 pp. Erotic Lesbian adventure story. ISBN 0-930044-88-6   8.95

PAZ by Camarin Grae. 336 pp. Romantic Lesbian adventurer with the power to change the world. ISBN 0-930044-89-4   8.95

SOUL SNATCHER by Camarin Grae. 224 pp. A puzzle, an adventure, a mystery — Lesbian romance. ISBN 0-930044-90-8   8.95

THE LOVE OF GOOD WOMEN by Isabel Miller. 224 pp. Long-awaited new novel by the author of the beloved *Patience and Sarah.* ISBN 0-930044-81-9   8.95

THE HOUSE AT PELHAM FALLS by Brenda Weathers. 240 pp. Suspenseful Lesbian ghost story. ISBN 0-930044-79-7   7.95

HOME IN YOUR HANDS by Lee Lynch. 240 pp. More stories from the author of *Old Dyke Tales.* ISBN 0-930044-80-0   7.95

PEMBROKE PARK by Michelle Martin. 256 pp. Derring-do and daring romance in Regency England. ISBN 0-930044-77-0   7.95

THE LONG TRAIL by Penny Hayes. 248 pp. Vivid adventures of two women in love in the old west. ISBN 0-930044-76-2   8.95

AN EMERGENCE OF GREEN by Katherine V. Forrest. 288 pp. Powerful novel of sexual discovery. ISBN 0-930044-69-X   9.95

THE LESBIAN PERIODICALS INDEX edited by Claire Potter. 432 pp. Author & subject index. ISBN 0-930044-74-6   12.95

DESERT OF THE HEART by Jane Rule. 224 pp. A classic; basis for the movie *Desert Hearts.* ISBN 0-930044-73-8   10.95

TORCHLIGHT TO VALHALLA by Gale Wilhelm. 128 pp. Classic novel by a great Lesbian writer. ISBN 0-930044-68-1   7.95

LESBIAN NUNS: BREAKING SILENCE edited by Rosemary Curb and Nancy Manahan. 432 pp. Unprecedented autobiographies of religious life. ISBN 0-930044-62-2   9.95

THE SWASHBUCKLER by Lee Lynch. 288 pp. Colorful novel set in Greenwich Village in the sixties. ISBN 0-930044-66-5   8.95

SEX VARIANT WOMEN IN LITERATURE by Jeannette Howard Foster. 448 pp. Literary history. ISBN 0-930044-65-7   8.95

These are just a few of the many Naiad Press titles — we are the oldest and largest lesbian/feminist publishing company in the world. Please request a complete catalog. We offer personal service; we encourage and welcome direct mail orders from individuals who have limited access to bookstores carrying our publications.